D1568971

# Winchester Pass

# Winchester Pass

## LAURAN PAINE

**Sagebrush**
Large Print Westerns

**Library of Congress Cataloging-in-Publication Data**

Paine, Lauran.
    Winchester pass / Lauran Paine.
        p.    cm.
    ISBN 1-57490-424-8 (lg. print : hardcover)


Library of Congress Cataloging-in-Publication Data was not
available at the time of publication.

Cataloging in Publication Data is available from
the British Library and the National Library of Australia.

**Sagebrush Large Print Westerns** are published in the United
States and Canada by Thomas T. Beeler, Publisher, PO Box 659,
Hampton Falls, New Hampshire 03844-0659. ISBN 1-57490-424-8

Published in the United Kingdom, Eire, and the Republic of
South Africa by Isis Publishing Ltd, 7 Centremead, Osney
Mead, Oxford OX2 0ES England. ISBN 0-7531-6689-5

Published in Australia and New Zealand by Bolinda Publishing
Pty Ltd, 17 Mohr Street, Tullamarine, Victoria, Australia, 3043
ISBN 1-74030-660-0


Manufactured by Sheridan Books in Chelsea, Michigan.

# Winchester Pass

# CHAPTER ONE

WHERE THE RISE OF MOUNTAINS MADE THEIR PURPLE thrust and where they pulled back to show a gash low down near the plain on either side, lay Winchester Pass. In years gone past an old trapper come near his last days had built a log shack near the crest and had exacted a toll from travelers, and in those times no one objected too strongly because the fee had been low and the old man had been colorful and strong in his prime; people had heard of him around a dozen camp fires and it was almost worth the toll just to look upon one of the old-time breed.

But he too passed away like the times which had molded and forged men like him, his log house lay crumbling in the summer sunlight all but forgotten, and now there were large cattle ranches south of Winchester Pass down in Tocannon Valley.

There weren't even very many men still around who recalled that originally the valley had been called Two-cannon, named for the brace of little bronze fieldpieces a soldier-column had once brought there, the first cannon the valley's Indian claimants had ever seen—or heard—and which had so successfully vanquished the warrior hordes.

But Time, they said, was a great healer, so all the violence and color of another era was lost in hazy yesterdays and nowadays men worked their ranges without fear of an arrow in the back or opening their eyes in their camps at dawn to find a dozen stalwart redskins standing there waiting to commence butchery upon awakened men still in their blankets.

1

What people neglected to mention, if they even understood it, was that Time was also the root of much evil, for there were many men to whom the passing of time was ignored and to whom yesterday was also today. These were the men who fought change with tooth and nail, who repudiated progress and clung to the old ways.

Men like Stuart Campbell who had come to the Tocannon country as a young man, tall and strong as an ox, with a half-wild way about him and a fierceness upon which his soul was impaled.

He had met the Indians head-on neither asking quarter nor giving it. He had created a legend for fighting prowess even the redskin warrior-race stood in awe of. The Utes called Stuart Campbell a Sioux and the Sioux called him a Comanche. In those early days the whites had shown him enormous respect, had gone to him for advice and judgments. He had taken up ten sections of Tocannon Valley land, brought in his herds, built up his buildings and had once, during an argument with old Red Kettle of the Utes, taken out his carbine, stepped down in front of Red Kettle and his fifty braves, drawn a line in the summertime dust and told the Utes if they ever crossed that line again he would wipe out their nation.

What had made that so extraordinary was that the day he'd hurled that bristling ultimatum to those warpath broncos, they had been fifty in number and Stuart Campbell had been entirely alone.

The marvel was that when he'd afterwards got back into the saddle, put up his gun, reined around and stiffly rode away, those Utes hadn't filled him so full of lead and arrows he'd have resembled a porcupine. Some wanted to, so the legend went, and it was probably true, but old Red Kettle had said no; that Campbell wasn't a normal man and if they killed him he'd come back in an evil form and bring a pestilence and a weakening to the tribes. The Utes never crossed that line again. In fact, their decline began shortly after that. They drifted further south down the Tocannon, more settlers came into the valley which Stuart Campbell had made safe, and eventually they just faded away.

And Time passed along spinning itself out through fecund springtimes, sunblasted summers and riotous, golden autumns. Each wintertime saw fewer Indians and more cowmen, saw more women and children and fatter herds grazing under the watchful eye of more rangeriders, and if old Stuart Campbell heeded this change at all, which was doubtful because he was busy from sunup to sundown, from earliest spring to latest winter, he gave no indication of it, for after all when a man's mighty log buildings are set squarely in the heartland of ten square miles of range, progress couldn't get any closer than that to him, and he wasn't aware of its coming.

The old man had married a Ute woman once, but she had died bearing his second child—a daughter—and since then he'd never sought another wife. But that daughter had grown to flowering womanhood taking up the slack, gradually, which had come to Tocannon Ranch after her mother's death.

Her name was Petl, the same as her mother. She was twenty-two years old and strikingly beautiful in her dusky, voluptuous way, and she was wise in the ways of men, had got that way long before leaving her teens because Tocannon Ranch hired six steady riders and during haying season had a round dozen working on the place. The presence of a beautiful girl brought out all

3

the hungers in lonely men. Petl had learned early how a man's mouth said one thing, his eyes another.

Her brother, at twenty-four, was the old man's second-in-command. His name was Brigham, an honorable name in Utah Territory when he'd been born, and he was a lot like old Stuart, but not in coloring. Where the old man was grizzled and fair with smoke-grey eyes and a Highland jaw, Brigham was dusky too, and rawboned, massively muscled and yet not so loud or blunt or fierce as his father. He was sometimes fatalistic, sometimes savage, but usually he was quiet and efficient without saying much.

But there was an iron bond between the father and his children. Once, a handsome stranger had ridden in on his way south astride a golden horse wearing a lashed-down pearl-handled .44 and Petl's heart had stood still when he smiled down at her. But afterwards when old Stuart had spoken a while with this man he had quietly saddled up and gone on, and Petl had listened to what the old man had to say.

"I know his kind, girl. He'd bring you nothing but heartache. Everything he has in his favor is on the outside; inside he's hollow and cold and calculating."

The stranger had never returned and if Petl had never quite forgotten him, at least she never again mentioned him.

And the years passed silently along leaving scarcely any trace of their passing. The Tocannon herds grew in size and numbers. Each autumn Brigham, his father and four of their steady riders trailed northward to rails-end with the steers and barren heifers, returned with laden pack animals and a cache of hoarded gold, and this was the only way any of them measured time, and that was their fatal mistake.

4

It was the tag-end of a rainy springtime with no one moving far from the home place that a man came down through Winchester Pass with two pack horses totally unobserved, wound his way six miles below Tocannon Ranch and set up camp against the west wall of the big valley on land well inside that mark old Stuart had drawn in the dust so many years earlier.

No one knew the stranger was camped down there until Cliff Lefton who'd been a Tocannon rider five years, came upon him shortly after the rainy season had passed and sat his horse dumbfounded as the leaned-down lanky stranger held up a tin cup from his cooking fire and said, "Coffee, mister? Raw weather like this a man needs something hot inside him."

Cliff had sat a long moment studying the stranger before deciding to accept. The man looked to be in his late twenties. He was a tall, loose-moving man with thick wrists and big hands. His shape tapered from big shoulders to the lean flanks of a horseman, and he smiled easily, but for all that there was something in his eyes that Cliff didn't miss; it was a poised, confident, almost a challenging look. He seemed to Cliff to be a person who made damned few mistakes, did nothing haphazardly, and wouldn't be likely to set up a permanent camp here on Tocannon land without knowing first where he was and what he was doing.

Cliff stamped up to the little fire. It was a raw day, one of those blustery ones when winter's last gasps were capable of chilling a man through his chaps and blanket-coat. And that coffee was good too. There was no sweetening for it but Cliff wasn't used to sweetening anyway, so he stood there bundled against the rawness, sipping, looking around at the stranger's tree-hung effects, studying the newcomer himself, and finally he said, "Mister; mind if I ask your name?"

The stranger stood across the fire. "Don't mind at all," he said pleasantly. "It's Russell Holmes."

Cliff sipped and nodded and said his own name, then he asked the next routine question. "You just passing through, Russ?"

And Holmes' expression smoothed out a little towards Cliff as though answering questions didn't sit too well with him—which it didn't. "Thought I'd stay a while, Cliff. The trails are kind of muddy this time of year. Besides, I like the Tocannon country."

"You been here before?"

"Yes. Four years back I helped bring in some cattle for a feller at the valley's lower end. I forget his name now. Ever since then I've remembered the place. Always thought it might be the place I'd settle down in some day. You know how it goes with a feller, Cliff; all of a sudden the yesterdays start catching up with a man."

"Yeah, I know," murmured Cliff, bent to put his tin cup down, straightened back up and put a grave gaze across at Russ Holmes. "But I'll tell you, Russ—this isn't the best place to make a permanent camp."

"Oh? Bears in the woods behind me, or lions?"

"No. There's bears and cougars but that's not what I had in mind. You see, this here is Campbell range; belongs to Stuart Campbell of Tocannon Ranch."

Holmes said, "The hell it does," and it sounded to Cliff as though he was being mocked. And Holmes faintly smiled too, which wasn't exactly what Cliff thought a man ought to do when he was being politely warned to get off. So Cliff began to cool out a little towards this stranger whom he'd initially felt like warming up to.

6

He said, "There's a good creek back in the hills a couple of miles with some little meadows along it. There's trout up there and grouse and what-not, an' if I was you I'd break this here camp and move on up into the forest to camp."

Russ stood there with his head dropped low while he silently and meticulously built a smoke. He raised his eyes only as he lit up, and he wasn't smiling any more. "You ever hear of the Soldiers' and Sailors' Bounty Act, Cliff?" he asked quietly.

"No," said Cliff, then corrected himself. "Well; I've *heard* of it, yes, but I don't know nothin' about it except what we was told last fall when we drove cattle the other side of Winchester Pass to rails-end, and all them clod-hoppers out there had taken up their land under it."

"Well," drawled Russ Holmes, "I'll tell you how it works, Cliff. If you'd been a soldier in the war, when you got discharged afterwards you could lay claim to a piece of unclaimed land. They have a big map of Utah Territory in the land officer up in Denver, along with maps of all the other territories, and you pick out the piece you want, file a claim, get it approved, then all you've got to do find your land, make the necessary improvements on it within two years, and it belongs to you."

"But the war was over a long while ago," said Cliff, beginning to have an uneasy feeling about this tall stranger and the dead-level way he had of looking straight through a man.

"Yes, it was, but a man can file any time. The only thing is, he can't file but once. You can understand why that is; there'd be fellers filing on good land, selling it for a big price and going back to file again."

Cliff let this go by. He hadn't been a soldier and he

7

wasn't interested in the Bounty Act anyway. What he *was* interested in was what Russ Holmes seemed to be telling him, and he said, "You got one of them land patents?"

"You're standing about two-thirds of the way inside it," replied the taller man, and flagged eastward with an upflung arm. "It runs from that little creek you were telling me about due east one mile, due south and north one mile."

Russ dropped his arm, narrowed his eyes against the rising smoke from his cigarette and exchanged a long look with Cliff Lefton without saying another word. His expression was knowing and tough.

Cliff's thoughts were troubled. He twisted half-way around to look out over the land, although he didn't really have to do this because he knew every foot of Tocannon range, had in fact been riding it summer and winter for five years. Still, he fixed the approximate boundaries of Holmes' claim in his mind while simultaneously speculating on what would ensue when he got back to the home place and repeated all this to old Stuart and the others.

"Well," he finally said, "thanks for the coffee. I'd better be on my way."

"You're welcome," responded Russ Holmes, hooking both thumbs in his shell-belt. "Any time you're down this way drop in. It's a lonely life, being a settler."

Cliff mounted, turned his horse and touched his hat. "I reckon it would be at that," he said, and loped away northward with the gusty wind working its way down under his collar. He didn't slow to a jog until he was two miles off and later, with the wind dying away along towards late afternoon, he approached the home place at a long-legged walk.

# CHAPTER TWO

STUART AND BRIGHAM LISTENED STOICALLY TO everything Cliff Lefton had to report while evening was settling over the valley and its rampart, surrounding high peaks. They were at the bunkhouse with the other men, waiting for Petl to ring the supper triangle, and the seven of them lounged and smoked and didn't have much to say for a long while after Cliff was finished. Eventually dark-eyed, bronzed-faced Joe Mesa said, "I reckon it was bound to happen some day. Remember all them other ones north of the Pass with their sections of land and their sod houses when we took the drive up to rails-end last Fall?"

Everyone remembered but except for a solemn nod here and there no one commented about this. Mostly, the men were watching old Stuart from beneath lowered hat-brims. It would be Stuart who said whatever had to be said about this trespassing, and who would institute whatever action was to be taken. They were loyal men, tough and hard as iron towards someone whom they considered a likely enemy. But they would not start anything by themselves, so they smoked and lounged and acted as though their entire interest lay only in the direction of the big kitchen over at the main house, while actually this wasn't what was in their minds at all.

But Stuart didn't say anything. He slouched along the little porch in front of the bunkhouse looking thoughtful and pensive. He lifted his smoke, drew inward, exhaled, and when Petl finally struck the triangle sending harsh but welcome music out over the yard, and for a mile onwards in all directions, he tossed down his smoke, stepped on it and said, "Time to eat."

Nothing more was said about the squatter on Tocannon's south range for several days. For one thing there was a lot of unpleasant birthing to look after; this was springtime when cows were calving, which wasn't much of a chore, but there were close to a thousand replacement heifers calving too this spring, and that *was* a chore. Not all first-calf heifers just lay down and had their calves. The blustery, alternately warm, alternately cold weather had something to do with it. All seven of them including old Stuart, were in the saddle from dawn 'til dusk. Confounded heifers always tried to hide when ready to calve, and that made it even harder on the men. First you had to find the danged animals, then, if they'd calved-out clean, the minute you stepped down to see was the calf all right, the blasted critters tried to gore you. And if they weren't all right, the calf was coming backwards or was hung-up, you could be there for two hours trying to pull the calf and avoid being skewered by an upset mother at the same time, with the result that invariably your otherwise sunny disposition, left you looking like a butcher, and feeling a lot less than a man.

But calving was a springtime chore. There was no way around it, and because all cows didn't calve at the same time, a man might spend nearly a full month doing nothing but riding and doing this unpleasant task.

There was another peril to this springtime occupation too. Since the cowboys rarely rode in pairs and each man was more or less upon his own, if anything happened an injured man could lie out behind a tree or in a brushy arroyo until evening when the other men returned to the ranch before it was known that he was missing. Many a gored range-rider had died in a big pool of his own blood between morning and evening, and also, more than a few had died because, finding a cow who was hiding, and being hurt in that same remote place, he hadn't been found for several days afterwards.

Calving-time was synonymous with springtime, and while winter-weary men were always relieved to feel the first good warmth again, see the emerald grass pushing up, sight those clean Vs of high-flying geese overhead bound for their summer feeding grounds, there was also the sober fact to be faced that once more it was calving-time, with all the grim and unpleasant ramifications this meant.

And this was a particularly bad spring too. Not entirely because Tocannon Ranch had an exceptionally large bunch of first-calf heifers to calve out, but also because the weather was not favorable. It still froze at night, warmed up during the day, was alternately hot and cold with blustery winds, which complicated things for the cattle. A good warm spring with no frost seemed always to coincide with an easy calving time, but as the Mexican, Joe Mesa, told Brigham when they met near day's-end on the trail home, "If a man could have everything he wanted in this life, it wouldn't be necessary for me to work for your paw, and it wouldn't be necessary for your paw to run cattle, because there would be cattle everywhere running loose for the taking, no?"

Brigham had smiled at that and shrugged. He was soiled from head to heel from the day's work. On the way in, with a failing big red sun over his left shoulder he'd idly thought that his mother's people had had the best of it. They didn't try to help a buffalo cow have her calf; they'd been content to allow Providence to take care of things like that. All they'd done was hunt the greasy-fat ones that survived, flesh the hides, jerk the meat, make their lodges and clothing from the hides,

11

and give thanks to their gods for a bountiful season.

In a way, what Mesa had said coincided perfectly with the Indian philosophy. But now the world was too settled, too complicated. Brigham accepted Joe's offer of a tobacco sack, worked up a puffy cigarette, returned the makings and looked on down the land towards the buildings. Something further out caught and held his attention. Smoke was rising straight up over against the foothills down there perhaps four, five miles southward. He pointed that out to Mesa. They rode along for a while looking and saying nothing, then the *vaquero* made a sage guess.

"Cliff's squatter, maybe. Falling trees and burning the slash." Mesa deeply inhaled, exhaled, and said, "A man cuts down trees to make a cabin. To build a barn or to make corrals."

Brigham's Indian-black eyes turned speculative towards that spiraling grey smoke but he still said nothing. In his father's own good time they would be told what to do.

Mesa looked around, considered the blunt jaw and the mighty shoulders Brigham had inherited from old Stuart, and he said, "One man is not so much. But unless we close off Winchester Pass there will be others. You remember how thick they were on the other side of the mountains?"

Brigham inclined his head, he remembered. Still, it was not his decision to make. No decision was ever his to make. Stuart did the thinking and the ordering, had always done it.

"I think pretty quick now your father will go down and throw that man off the land."

Brigham finally spoke, saying, "When I was a kid an old buck told me once how it was when the first whites

12

came. He said the Indians killed them. More came and they killed them too. Then still more came, and things began going the other way; the whites began killing the Indians."

"Well," said Mesa, killing his smoke atop the saddlehorn, "life is seldom mild, Brig."

But that wasn't the point, at least it wasn't in Brigham's mind, and he proved it when he went on speaking. "Maybe that's happening again, Joe. Maybe the old man'll kill this one; maybe we'll ride against the next one or two that come into Tocannon Valley. But what happens maybe a year or two from now when fifteen or twenty come here?"

"How can they do that?" inquired the Mexican. "There's not that much free land in here. How can they do that unless they want to fight us for this land?"

"We fought the Indians for it, didn't we, and it was their land too?"

Mesa shook his head adamantly. "That wasn't the same, *amigo*. They didn't really *own* the land, they just camped on it, and moved on."

"Yeah? Joe; this squatter of Cliff's—he said he had some kind of a claim on Tocannon range, didn't he? Well; someone's got to be wrong. Either my paw's got title or this stranger has; can't both of 'em have title to the same piece of land. And Joe . . ."

"Yes?"

"Suppose my paw's title is no better than the Indian's title was; what then?"

Such an idea was preposterous to Joe Mesa, the lifelong *arriero* and cowboy. Always, the powerful and rich and strong, had title to land. Who would dare ever question such a thing? But still and all, Brigham had brought up a disquieting line of thought. Suppose, in

13

fact, old Stuart Campbell *could* be dispossessed; where would that leave Joe Mesa, Cliff Lefton, the other loyal, permanent riders?

"I think," said Joe darkly, "your father shouldn't wait too long in this matter. I think he should go down there one of these nice dark nights and get rid of that squatter."

They rode on into the ranch yard and discovered that the others were already there ahead of them, including Cliff who'd been detailed the south range. While they off-saddled there was the usual ripple of rangemen's talk at the barn, and afterwards while they lounged around upon the bunkhouse porch and steps more recitals of the day's doings were passed about.

Cliff said the squatter had peeled some logs, had pegged out where he meant to build his log-house, had even finished one small corral for his three horses already. Old Stuart was not with them this evening. He was over at the house working on tallies, so he missed this information, but the other men eyed Brigham thinking that in his father's absence the younger Campbell would speak for the ranch-interests.

But Brigham sat there with his tired back to an upright post and never said a word, so after a while when Cliff had exhausted his particular topic of the long-legged stranger, the conversation drifted along to other matters until Petl rang the triangle and they all got up, dusted off their breeches and trooped on over towards the big kitchen.

Stuart was there at the table ahead of them lost in thought and since Cliff nor any of the others felt like bringing up the subject of their particular squatter again, it was not commented upon.

They kidded Petl a little which was their custom and

14

teased her about the coffee, which was black as ink and strong enough to float a horseshoe, saying it wasn't strong enough. But she was equal to all this, since she'd come to womanhood around these men and others just like them, and returned as good as she got.

Only Stuart didn't join in any of this, but then he rarely did anyway. Not that old Stuart didn't possess his own rough sense of humor—he did—but as the years passed along he showed it more rarely.

This particular evening he ate and drank and afterwards left the table to stroll outside for a smoke. Since he'd started eating sooner he was finished before the others, and also since, like many of the big ranches, smoking was not allowed in the main house, he exacted from himself the same obedience to this old rule that he also exacted from his men.

Later, as the others drifted out, he spoke to Joe Mesa, drawing the only Mexican cowboy in Tocannon Valley to one side where those two stood solemnly speaking back and forth as the other men drifted on along towards the bunkhouse for their nightly poker session. Brigham drifted along too, but not before he'd looked over and seen his father and Mesa together in the shadows at the side of the house.

But if Brigham thought anything of this it didn't show on his face. But then, few emotions showed openly on Brigham's face at any time, unless a person looked very closely and even then it would show only upon certain occasions, such as when Stuart told him to do something which Brigham had his own opinions about doing.

But there was never any hint of rebellion at Tocannon Ranch. There never had been, not even in the early days when tasks had been less routine and sometimes

15

connected with violence, because old Stuart gave an order and if it was not instantly obeyed, the dissenter went riding down the trail the following morning with all his belongings behind the saddle. A man could mellow in some respects as age gentled him, but men like Stuart Campbell never mellowed towards the solidest convictions they possessed, and with old Stuart obedience was the heart and sinew of ruling men on a big cow outfit.

It was clear too, the longer he and Joe Mesa talked, that Stuart was making pronouncements, because Joe only asked a few questions and after that he simply listened and nodded.

Joe too was a man with convictions. The fact that his beliefs happened to coincide with the identical beliefs of Stuart Campbell made what he now had to do that much easier for him to appreciate.

# CHAPTER THREE

CLIFF LEFTON WAS DETAILED TO THE SOUTH RANGE again, which he didn't really object to for the elemental reason that there weren't very many calvy heifers down there. And Cliff had another reason for not objecting too; he enjoyed sitting back in the westward forest spying on Russ Holmes.

He had nothing against Holmes, in fact as he watched the knowledgeable way the tall man worked, Cliff began to have some admiration for him.

But the morning he rode down there and found no sign of Holmes he recalled seeing Joe Mesa and old Stuart talking the evening before over by the main house, and he didn't have to do a lot of mental labor to

16

come up with the possible reason Holmes wasn't around.

Still, a man minded his own business, remembered his manners, did what he was told and kept his mouth closed, and barring accidents he should live to reach sixty. But Cliff had his share of raw curiosity too, so he rode on up to Holmes' camp and sat his saddle gazing around.

The axe was there leaning upon a sapling. The saw and sledge and two red wedges were also there, so Holmes hadn't begun felling and splitting. Two things that *weren't* there were Holmes' six-gun in its holster and his Winchester saddle gun.

He could have gone hunting. He could even have decided not to split logs today and just do a little exploring into the westerly mountains. The trouble with that was simply that all three of Holmes' horses were idly swishing their tails in that shady little corral he'd built for them, and no horseman ever went exploring on foot.

Cliff swung down, walked on over and peered at the stone-ring where Holmes always did his cooking. He was putting forth his right hand to feel the coffee pot, when a soft-drawling voice came out of the rearward trees to freeze Cliff in his tracks.

"It's still warm, help yourself."

Cliff drew stiffly upright and turned. Holmes was striding towards him out of the gloomy forest back there. He had his gun-belt around him and was carrying his Winchester. He wasn't smiling.

"Go ahead, fill up both cups, Cliff. I missed breakfast this morning so I'll join you."

There was something bleak in the big man's gaze as he came on up alongside Cliff, something cold and

17

watchful. Holmes said, "How come you to ride right on in this morning, Cliff, when yesterday and the day before that you sat back up in the trees just watching?"

Cliff's face burnt red. He ducked his head and bent to fill the coffee cups. It rankled that his secret vigil hadn't been secret at all. He felt like a small boy who has just been caught stealing apples.

"Wondered where you were," he mumbled, twisted and held up one of the cups. "That's all; just wondered if you were around."

"Why should you wonder that, Cliff?" asked Russ Holmes with his dead-level gaze fixed upon Lefton. "Were you worried about me, maybe?"

"No, I wasn't worried. Just curious I reckon."

"Like you were curious yesterday and the day before?"

Cliff sipped lukewarm coffee avoiding Holmes' stare. He didn't answer. He didn't feel comfortable here and wished he'd gone out and around this blasted place.

"Or were you wondering if Joe had done his work?"

Cliff nearly choked on a gulletful of coffee. He cleared his throat and spat aside. "Joe who?" he said, and instantly realized how inane that had sounded.

"Joe Mesa, the feller who came sneaking up on me last night. At least he said his name was Mesa—before I buried him."

Cliff's discomfort vanished. He looked across at Russ Holmes out of big eyes; "Buried—him . . .?"

"Yeah. I guess you wouldn't have known about that though, because there were no shots fired to carry on up to Campbell's place." Holmes flagged off towards the forest he'd recently emerged from. "Buried Joe up in the trees about a mile, Cliff, in one of those nice little grassy meadows up there."

Cliff didn't finish his coffee. He put the cup down carefully and stood up again. He kept watching Holmes, kept watching the bigger man's dark blue eyes and his quirked-up lips; kept listening to the unperturbed softness of his steady masculine voice.

"He made a foolish mistake, Cliff. He rode a shod horse and I heard him twenty minutes before he crept up here in his stocking-feet with his knife. When he lunged for my blankets of course I wasn't there. I was behind him. In the scuffle he lost the knife, I got it, and . . ." Russ rolled up his shoulders in a fatalistic shrug. "You know, before he died he got pretty talkative. Did you know he was raised down in Arizona?"

"No," whispered Cliff.

"He sure enough was. And he rode for some of the best outfits down along the border too; outfits like Mexican Hat, Texas Star, Lerdo Brothers." Holmes flung away the dregs and tossed aside the cup. "Did you know he was to get a bonus for socking me away last night?"

Cliff didn't answer this time, he simply wagged his head. He'd ridden with Joe Mesa a long time. Had shared blankets with him on the autumn drives. Had bellied up to the cow-town bars with him.

"Yeah. Joe was promised fifty dollars to carve out my heart, Cliff. Tell you what; you go on back and tell old Stuart Campbell he owes me for two tricks now, owes me for you spying on me and for Joe trying to cut my throat. You tell him for me, Cliff, that I'm a peaceable man. You tell him that if he's too damned old or too damned yellow to do his own dirty work, not to send any more fools to do it for him, because the next Tocannon man I find inside my boundary lines I'll plant deep down right beside Joe."

19

Cliff had his gun on but it never occurred to him to try and use it. For one thing Russ Holmes wasn't making anything personal out of this between them. In fact, he was as pleasant-seeming, as courteous and hospitable as he always was when Cliff rode in. But there was another reason for Cliff to stand easy too; Joe Mesa had been one of the most resourceful, tough men Cliff had ever known, and here stood his killer without a mark on him, looking not the least bit upset after encountering Joe. It struck Cliff Lefton that *this* was no ordinary squatter at all.

Then Holmes stepped back, leaned his Winchester upon a log and cocked his head over to Cliff. "Care for some breakfast?" he asked. Then he said apologetically, "I know it's kind of late, but I couldn't get to it any sooner." And he smiled at Cliff.

No thought was further from Cliff Lefton's mind right then than eating. "No, thanks," he muttered past stiff lips. "You sure Joe was dead when you buried him?"

"Plumb sure, Cliff. If he was a friend of yours I'm sorry. But a man's got a right to defend himself according to my beliefs."

Holmes hunkered by his stone-ring, poked in the oak ashes until he'd turned up some live coals, then he carefully placed twigs atop them and used his hat to fan a small flame to brisk life. While he was doing this he ignored Cliff completely, until Cliff's right arm moved. Then he raised those dark blue eyes and gently shook his head.

"Don't try it," he said. "You'd never get it done. Besides that I don't like killing and two of 'em the same day'd ruin my feelings."

"I wasn't goin' to draw," said Cliff, telling the candid

20

truth. "I was reaching for my sack of makings."

Holmes smiled. It made his whole face look different, younger, more boyish, more warm and friendly. All but those dark, violet eyes; they didn't change at all from their way of spearing through a man.

"Go ahead," he said. "Have your smoke." He rummaged in a pocket, brought forth a gold watch on a heavy gold chain, a shiny old buckskin poke that jangled with silver when Holmes shook it, and he stood up holding these things forth. "Joe's," he said. "Take 'em back with you. I'll keep the knife and guns as sort of payment on a bad debt."

Cliff forgot all about the smoke. He took the poke, the watch and chain and visibly swallowed. He recognized them, particularly that watch on its massive gold chain, which had been Mesa's pride and joy.

"Guess," he muttered, gazing at Mesa's effects, "I'd better be drifting along."

Holmes didn't say anything. He watched Cliff turn and step up over leather. He was gravely watching the younger cowboy, waited until Cliff had pocketed Mesa's things and had evened up his reins, then he said, "Cliff; the next time stay out of the trees back there. You're welcome at the camp any time. Just don't pull some bonehead stunt like skulkin' up on me because I have a feeling that from now on there won't be any more spyin'—only shooting."

Cliff nodded understanding, eased his horse out in a walk and passed on over the countryside sitting stiff in the saddle, sitting awkwardly up there as though extremely conscious of what a handsome target his back made.

He got back to the home place two hours ahead of the others and put up his horse, made a shaky smoke in

21

front of the barn and was leaning there upon the hitchrack when Petl came along and showed surprise at his being in so early. Without a word he drew forth Mesa's buckskin poke, watch and chain, and held them out for the lovely girl to see.

"He killed Joe. Killed him with his own knife and buried him in the forest."

Petl knew that watch also. She stood stock-still looking incredulous. "Who killed Joe?" she whispered.

"Russ Holmes. That squatter on the south range. He just give me this stuff along with a message for your paw. He was as cool and polite as though nothing had happened."

Petl, who knew men, caught the full impact of Cliff's numbness, felt the shock and saw the bewilderment in the young cowboy. "He found those things," she said. "He was making a joke with you, Cliff. Why would he kill Joe? Where would they meet and . . ." Her voice trailed off as a new look appeared in the cowboy's eyes; a knowing, secretive look. Her voice altered, became quieter and harder towards him. "What was Joe doing down there, Cliff? What happened between them that we don't know about?"

But Cliff had his convictions too, and keeping a closed mouth was one of them. He dropped his smoke, ground it out and shook his head at her. "I don't know anything about it, Petl. All I know is what he told me to tell your paw—an' what he said about Joe. That's all."

"Well. What *did* he say about Joe?"

"I don't want to talk about it. I'll tell your paw an' if he wants you to know *he* can tell you."

She watched the numbness begin to pass, saw the solid shock of a friend's passing begin to dissipate to be replaced by a rawer look in Cliff Lefton's face. She

22

knew that look; she'd seen it before on the faces of men. She turned and started on across the yard.

The afternoon passed slowly. It was a fine clear day with good warmth steadily building up, a handsome azure sky overhead, and the scent of new growth in the benign air. It was a hell of a day for a man to be buried on.

Cliff went over to the bunkhouse with listless steps. He went back in his mind over the times, the high spots in his life, when he and Joe Mesa had been together. And later on, he recalled Russ Holmes, and despite his increasing feeling of indignation and loss, he couldn't quite bring himself to hate the stranger, and that troubled him too. A man should always hate the slayer of his friends. But he recalled Holmes, not as a deceptive man at all, nor as a swaggering gunman, but instead as a frank-faced person with a good smile and a quiet way of speaking; as a tough, capable, confident man, but not as a killer or a bully or a fool.

Certainly not as a fool. No fool ever could have caught Joe Mesa from behind and killed Joe with his own knife.

Holmes emerged in Cliff's thoughts exactly as he was. As a strange man perhaps, and with eyes that saw much more than other men ordinarily saw and a litheness which was half-masked by his cool deliberateness—like when he'd seen Cliff's arm move and had looked up at him, had warned him against drawing. But he also thought Holmes had made a very fatal mistake in killing Joe Mesa. Not that old Stuart felt any greater regard for Joe than for any of his other Tocannon riders, but simply because it was a law of the range country that an employer backed his men to the limit. Old Stuart had been one of the originators of laws

23

like that. He'd never overlook the killing of one of his men. Especially not, thought Cliff without any feelings about this one way or the other, since he had himself sent Joe down there to sock away that squatter.

He was still sitting there on the bunkhouse porch with Joe's poke and watch in his hands when the others began drifting in. They saw him and he saw them, but for as long as it took them to off-saddle and splash in the barn-trough getting off the grime and sweat of this long day, they didn't stroll on over.

And the last pair to approach were old Stuart and his powerful-built, dusky son. They had ridden together today but because neither was talkative they could have been miles apart and it wouldn't have made any difference as far as exchanging ideas and methods were concerned.

Cliff let all the others stamp up onto the porch before he held out the things in his hand to old Stuart, and tonelessly made his dispassionate report. Every man there except Stuart, was totally shocked. Stuart only gazed at the watch, the gold chain, the buckskin pouch, and stood loose and easy and expressionless until Cliff had finished. Then he lifted his eyes and showed them all a wildness lying deep down in their depths, turned and hiked on over towards the house without uttering a sound.

# CHAPTER FOUR

FIRST THINGS CAME FIRST. THE FOLLOWING DAY ONE of the riders—Martin Crabb—got bucked off at the corrals in one of those freak accidents which sometimes happened, and this kept any of the others from knowing right then why Stuart had assembled them at the barn to all ride off together instead of singly.

Crabb was riding a Morab colt in the hackamore; had been riding this particular three-year-old for ten days now and the pony had been coming right along. But this particular morning the pony was guyed-up, and when a stupid barn-owl chose that precise moment to flop out of the barn-loft in ungainly flight making its raucous squawk, Martin's colt had fired with him, had got its head down before Martin had any idea what was happening, and had gone off sideways in a wild series of sun-fishing bucks. For a few moments Martin, a pretty fair hand, had struggled to remain aboard, which was his big mistake, for if the colt had thrown him out in the yard he probably wouldn't have been injured. But Martin fought to get his balance, fought to ride out the wild storm, and as the colt came even with the log-barn and had violently whipped around, Martin had been thrown against those unrelenting big logs with considerable force.

Brigham said later he heard Martin's skull pop against wood like a rotten melon being dashed against a rock. Cliff Lefton got over there first, knelt and straightened Martin out upon the ground. There was a trickle of blood dripping from the unconscious man's nose, and later, as they made a pallet of two blankets to get him into the bunkhouse, blood began to trickle from both ears as well.

They removed Martin's boots, his gun-belt, his hat, and they also opened his shirt and slackened off his belt. He was breathing, but it was a fluttery kind of very shallow breathing which made each of them, as they stood crowding around the bunk, think Martin Crabb was done for.

25

Brigham went after his sister and some hot water. Petl had a way with injuries and her hands were gentle. She worked until a little before noon making Martin comfortable and wiping away that leaking blood, then it stopped and Martin's breathing became a little stronger.

She found the cracked place on Martin's skull and showed it to Stuart, saying, "He should have a doctor."

Stuart gazed downward and said, "What could a doctor do that lying here without moving won't do for him, Petl? Besides, if we tried moving him it could be fatal."

"You don't have to move him, Paw. All you have to do is send someone outside to bring back a doctor."

But Stuart shook his head over this too. "It'd take three days; by then he'll be either dead or on the mend."

There was truth in what old Stuart said, but right then it didn't sit too well with the others, the way he made his grim pronouncements. But that was old Stuart's way; he saw to the heart of things and called a spade a spade. If there was any sentiment in him, he didn't show it now. "One of you will have to stay with him all the time, day and night. If he gets feverish he'll roll around and maybe lash out. You'll have to keep him quiet and watch that he doesn't hit his head on the wall or the back of his bunk."

Petl stepped back. "I'll fix some herbs," she murmured, watching the unconscious cowboy, seeing how his face was purpling, beginning to swell and turn lumpy. "I'll put enough laudanum in it to keep him out so he won't thresh around." Then she turned and walked on out of the bunkhouse.

The rest of them stood around at loose ends expecting old Stuart to detail all but one or two of them to go on back to work. But he never did. He stood like a stone

26

statue watching Martin Crabb for a long time and when he eventually turned away he said, "Brig, you come with me."

It was close to high noon now; the caring for Martin Crabb had killed half the day. Petl was heading on across the yard and saw her father and brother at the hitchrack ready to ride out, and called over to them.

"Dinner'll be ready in fifteen minutes."

Stuart looked around as she moved on towards the bunkhouse with her mug of hot herb tea and didn't answer, just sat up there watching. When she stepped inside he turned his horse, jerked his head at Brigham, and rode northward out and around the mighty log-barn where they were concealed from sight, then he changed course completely and struck out due south, but bearing always over towards the forested rim of the valley's west side.

Brigham said nothing. He thought he knew their destination the moment old Stuart altered course like that. He also thought he understood why they had kept the barn between them and the bunkhouse too; if none of the others saw which way they rode off, then later on no one could actually say they'd seen anything at all.

Range-law wasn't book-law, and if things sometimes had to be done which didn't gibe with legal-writ, then they had to be accomplished quietly, but that didn't mean they were illegal, at least not in the eyes of the men who did them and who believed that their own law was best for them, while book-law was best for others, mainly city-folks who'd always had book-law to protect them. Maybe times *had* changed, maybe there was law in the land now, but one thing was quite certain in Tocannon Valley, the law was many miles away, like the doctors also were, and when immediate action had to be taken someone had to take it. Brigham believed this as firmly as his father had all his life believed it, but still, a generation of living separated these two and while one believed as the other also believed, there was a difference here too. A man no longer drew a line in the dust and threatened extermination to anyone crossing it. *That* arbitrary kind of law was, in Brigham's eyes at least, a thing of the past.

But he rode along, silent as usual, silent and thoughtful and expressionless, waiting to come to the end of this ride. He knew where it would end even before his father left the shielding trees in full view of a half-built log-house where a lanky man was working with his back to them upon the chinking of a mud-wattle fireplace.

Brigham saw that man turn suddenly while they were still a long way out, watch them for a while, then step down, step around inside his walled-up house and emerge moments later with a carbine hooked in one arm. He had never before seen this man although he knew his name, and when his father hauled down to a slow walk the last two hundred yards Brigham made a close study of Russ Holmes. Old Stuart also was making a careful appraisal. He hadn't said a word since leaving home, but now he quietly spoke.

"Watch him, Brig. If he killed Joe Mesa in a fair fight he's no ordinary range-rider. Watch him close, boy."

Brigham would have done that anyway because he was curious about that lanky man whose searching gaze remained unwaveringly upon them until the old man halted fifty feet off, then made a slow little dragging circuit of the rearward plain as though expecting to find other men out there.

"I'm Stuart Campbell," said the old man quietly and

28

coldly. "You'll be Russell Holmes."

The lanky man gravely nodded without speaking. His build, in Brigham's view, was tough and sinewy and deceptively powerful. It tapered from shoulder points to lean flanks. The stare Holmes put outwards to them was candid, unafraid, and deadly without actually looking angry or belligerent.

"You sent me a message," said old Stuart.

"I did. I said unless you were too old or too yellow to do your own killing, you'd better not send any more boys on a man's errand."

"Big talk, Mister Holmes."

"The only kind you understand, Mister Campbell."

"A man sometimes mellows in his late years, Mister Holmes. Clear out of here. Pack up and ride on. I'm giving you the benefit of the doubt about Joe Mesa. Maybe you killed him in fair fight and maybe you didn't, but I'm giving you the benefit of the doubt in that."

Holmes shifted his stance and lay his carbine across his upper body, holding it with both hands. He said, "If you'd thought that through you'd never have said you'd give me the benefit of any doubt, because when a man has been sent out to kill another man, any way the other man can kill his assassin *is* a fair fight. And Mister Campbell—about that fifty dollar bonus you promised Mesa to cut my throat—give it to the next church you ride by. It won't make your lousy soul any cleaner but at least it'll be spent in a better cause than it was meant to be spent for."

Holmes glanced at Brigham, sought something in the younger man's expressionless, black gaze which was not there, and put his attention back upon the older man. "As for pulling out, Mister Campbell, forget it. I've got

29

a patent to this land. I've got improvements to make then it's mine."

"Maybe you'll never complete those improvements, Mister Holmes."

Russ gently wagged his head. "Don't make threats. At least not unless you've got your hand on a gun, Mister Campbell. I don't think you want me for an enemy."

"No? Don't you think I've had enemies like you before?"

Russ wagged his head again. "I know you haven't, Mister Campbell, and I'll tell you why. I'm not some blanket-Indian or some left-over trapper. I've got a right to do what I've started here; the U.S. Marshal, the U.S. Army, even the sheriff of the county and the courts will uphold my right."

"If you're dead, Mister Holmes?"

"Like I just said, Mister Campbell, don't make threats."

Old Stuart's flinty gaze was icy. "I never make threats," he said, "I make promises."

Holmes stepped back, turned and leaned his carbine against the raw, partially completed side-wall of his house. He straightened back around facing old Stuart and Brigham. "I told Cliff the next Tocannon men I caught trespassing down here I'd plant up in the forest beside Joe Mesa. Maybe you thought that was just talk. Well, you're wrong, Mister Campbell, *dead* wrong. You want a fight—here it is. Don't worry about the odds, two like you don't measure up to much of a man anyway, so go ahead and make your play any time you're ready. Go ahead and draw, both of you!"

Old Stuart didn't move. Neither did his son. They sat out there staring at Holmes, thinking their different

30

thoughts. Brigham was impressed by the squatter's courage, by his solid confidence. Old Stuart thought differently about Holmes; he thought there could be no question of warning this one off; he measured the stance, the level gaze, the cut-away holster at Holmes' hip and made his decision on the spot. He would bring in a professional to kill this one.

"The longer you think about it, Mister Campbell, the harder it is to do. Just make your draw, both of you, and take your chances. You want to get rid of me—you'll never have a better chance."

"No," said old Stuart shaking his head at Holmes, "as I told you, age mellows a man."

"Not a man like you it doesn't."

"Yes, a man like me. I'll tell you frank-out how it's going to be, Mister Holmes. Your horses will be run off, that log-house you're building—one night it'll catch fire and burn to the ground. Your cache of food will disappear, and finally, you'll *walk* out of Tocannon Valley without even your guns. I don't have to draw on you. I don't even have to hire you killed if I don't want to. But I might have that done too. Mister Holmes, these aren't threats. Like I said before—they're promises. And I keep my word, Mister Holmes."

Holmes' shoulders drooped a little when he saw this was not going to end in a blaze of gunfire. He looked steadily at old Stuart with scorn showing. He looked on over to Brigham. "If this old devil's your paw, tell me something—how can you respect a man who'd fight like that—burning a man out, stealing his horses?"

Brigham spoke for the first time with his direct and simple logic. "It's better than being shot down, isn't it, Mister Holmes? You can find another homestead."

It seemed they had each of them said all that had to

31

be said now, and for a moment they simply gazed at one another. Then Russ shrugged and stepped back to lean upon his half-finished wall. "Whatever else you are, Campbell, you speak right out, an' I reckon that might be some kind of a virtue, so I'll do the same. All right; you bring in your professional gunman to do what you're afraid of doing. I'll be right here waiting for him. And when you run off my three horses—I'll run off fifty of yours. And as for burning me out . . ." Holmes made a sardonic little smile with his lips. "Think that one over a long time before you try it, because I think your buildings are a lot older than mine, and therefore they'll be a lot dryer." When he stopped speaking that little iron-like smile still lingered down around his lips. "We understand each other, don't we, Mister Campbell?"

"Better than you think," agreed old Stuart flintily. "You're one man. All it takes for one man is one bullet. I've got a half-dozen men and I'll hire that many more —and offer a bigger bonus—if I have to."

"To keep one lousy section of rangeland?"

Stuart nodded. "I've had to do it before, Holmes, many times. You aren't the first to try and squat on Tocannon land."

Holmes sighed as he quietly considered old Stuart. He softly shook his head. "You're twenty years behind the times," he said, the roughness leaving his voice. "If you get me there'll be others. Maybe not this year but next year and the years after. If you kill them all the soldiers'll come, the law will come. You can't fight everyone. If you try it they'll wipe you out, they'll bury you, and maybe along with you they'll bury your son."

"I'll hold what is mine, Holmes. Don't worry about that. I've held it before and against bigger odds than you know." Old Stuart's gaze wavered, flicked out over the

32

log-house, the pole corrals, the litter and debris of a squatter-camp. "By this time next year there won't be a trace of any of this. Come on, Brig, let's head back."

Holmes stood watching. For as long as the Campbells were in sight he didn't move, but afterwards, with dusk marching steadily down the land, he picked up his Winchester and heavily strode back inside his partially completed house.

# CHAPTER FIVE

OLD STUART LEFT BRIGHAM IN CHARGE AND RODE ON out of the valley saying he was going to the settlements after a doctor for Martin Crabb, and also for more laudanum and other things they needed along that line, for it was the custom for those insular big ranches to be as nearly self-sufficient as they could be.

Brigham was there at the barn when his father rode out. Those two exchanged a somber nod. Petl came along shortly after the old man had departed and leaned upon the rack beside her brother.

"What else is he going after?" she asked.

And Brigham answered in his minimal, blunt way. "A gunman."

"To avenge Joe Mesa, Brig?"

"Naw. It's the land, Sis. And the way that stranger talked up to him. Called on us both to draw and fight it out."

"What's he like, Brig?"

"Oh; like most men I reckon. Maybe a little taller, a little ruggeder." Brigham paused, thought a while, then said, "No; he's *not* like other men. At least not like the ones you and I have known. When paw said we'd burn

33

him out he never batted an eye; he said if we tried that he'd burn *us* out. He even asked me how I could respect a man who hired his fighting done for him."

Brigham picked at a sliver of wood, worried it loose and put it between his teeth as he lifted his dark gaze and squinted far out where old Stuart was barely visible.

Petl watched Brigham's quiet, pensive expression for a while. She obviously wanted him to talk, to say more about the stranger. But Brigham had a quiet indifference that seemed at times to cover him completely. At least he always gave the impression of having such an air, unless—and Petl had seen this happen two or three times since they'd been children—unless someone pushed Brigham beyond the limits of good judgment. Then her brother wasn't the same man at all.

"Can you?" she softly asked.

"Can I what?"

"Respect a man who hires his fighting done for him."

Brigham brought his gaze down and around. He regarded his sister for a long time as though something about her had just occurred to him; as though he'd never before thought she would question old Stuart's decisions. He said, "A general doesn't take up a gun and go down into the lines during a war, Petl. He doesn't have to. He isn't even supposed to." And went on chewing that wood splinter and looking at her. "He's been fightin' for half a century to hold what we got. He's an old man now. It'd be foolish for him to try and draw against a feller like that Russ Holmes."

"But it's all right for him to burn Holmes out, run off his horses, hire a killer to come into the valley and bushwhack him?"

Brigham chewed and looked at the ground and didn't say anything.

34

"This is a huge valley, Brig."

"It wouldn't be if maybe fifty like him came in here and took up land, Petl."

"There's not that much unclaimed land for them to take up."

"How do you know that?"

"Well; the other ranches . . ."

"That's not it, Sis. I don't think Paw's got legal title to *our* land. I doubt if the other old-timers have title to their land either. Fifty years back you just rode in, carved out what you wanted, and fought all-comers to keep it." Brigham spat out the splinter. There was a vertical line between eyebrows. "You help keep the books; have you ever seen any land deeds?"

Petl's gaze turned thoughtful and after a moment she shook her head. "I don't think so. I don't recall anything like a land title." She drew up off the rack and started away.

Brigham watched her cross the yard and he faintly smiled. In all the things his sister did she was honest and usually transparent. She would go now directly to the office in the rear of the house and search for land deeds.

"Hey, Brig!"

He turned. It was Cliff Lefton over on the bunkhouse porch. "What."

"Martin's dope is wearing off. He's mumbling and throwin' himself around."

"Well, don't stand out on the porch," called back Brigham as he turned away from the hitchrack. "Go on in there and hold him steady."

Cliff ducked inside and Brigham continued on over towards the bunkhouse. His stride was checked up by the sound of horsemen. He turned, made out three of the regular riders swinging in from the east, and hurried along to the bunkhouse.

Martin was both delirious and feverish. They got some of the laudanum water down him, put wet rags across his forehead, then Brigham stood up as Crabb's writhings diminished. Young Cliff blew out a big sigh. "Scairt hell out of me," he muttered. "Maybe you better go get your sister. I'm no good at this doctoring business unless it's a horse or a cow."

Brigham went out as far as the porch and halted out there. His private opinion was that Martin Crabb was going to die. Where his head had struck the barn logs there was a sunken place which even the swelling couldn't conceal. As the men who had ridden in a while back emerged from the barn heading along towards the bunkhouse Brigham stepped down into the yard because he didn't feel like becoming involved in a long and fruitless discussion about Crabb.

He walked on over to the house, entered, went through the big kitchen and on into a little cubbyhole room which served as his father's office. There, he found Petl looking small at the desk with piles of old records around her.

He said, "Martin's coming around."

She nodded up at him, her eyes distant and pensive. "All right. Did you give him some more of the herb water?"

He nodded, watching her expression, wondering about that far-away look. He leaned there in the doorway. "Find anything?"

She picked up an old, yellowish, long piece of paper with old Stuart's cramped, tight scrawl covering all one side of it, gazed at it, then passed it over as she got up and walked on out of the room.

Brigham strained to read that scrawl, was still reading

36

it a half-hour later when Petl returned and after throwing him a look, went to work out in the kitchen. He turned finally, went out to her and held out the paper.

"It's some kind of a treaty with the Utes," he said, sounding wry. "But I can't make it out very well."

She spoke briskly with her back to him while she worked. "It's more than just a treaty, it's a gift of our land from Red Kettle in exchange for father's promise never to lead soldiers against the Utes."

Brigham scowled over the faded writing. "Then it's a deed," he said, and his expression lost some of its gravity. "It means we own the land."

Petl went on working saying nothing. There were shadows in the room with them, and a lengthening silence elsewhere which seemed to run on and on and on.

"That's a load off my mind, Sis."

"Is it? But are those old things recognized?"

Brigham thought about this. It seemed logical to him for such a deed as this to be perfectly legal. Certainly in the eyes of rangemen it would be considered legal.

"Why wouldn't it be?" he asked her.

"I don't know. I don't know anything about things like that and neither do you. But suppose father has this Russ Holmes put off—and some government-man comes along some day and says our title's no good either."

"Well; what of it?"

Petl turned. "You said Holmes might be killed, Brig. Is it right to kill a man over something you have no right to control in the first place?"

Brigham waved the paper. "This gives Tocannon Ranch control enough for me, Sis."

37

"To kill a man over a section of land, Brig?"

"I don't have to make that decision, Sis. Paw's already made it for us."

She kept her liquid dark gaze upon him for a moment then slowly turned back to her work, and later, when he spoke on, she ignored him completely. He put the paper back upon old Stuart's desk, left the house and sauntered on down where the other men were lounging upon the bunkhouse porch. When he came up one of them said, "Martin's better now. Miss Petl sure has a way to her."

Brigham eased down upon a vacant porch step. "Find any more heifers in trouble?" he asked.

One man said he had, in fact, found two more, but the other men said the calving season had to be just about over and done with because they hadn't found anything abnormal out on the range at all.

"But I went south a few miles," said one cowboy casually, "and seen that squatter-feller. You fellers'd never guess what he was doing. Sittin' on a stump out in plain sight splittin' shake-shingles neat as a whistle. Every time that axe rose and fell, there was a shake near two feet long."

Brigham felt around for his tobacco sack. "You ride on in?"

"Nossir," said the cowboy. "When a man sends out word he don't want company, I just naturally don't go callin' on him."

Cliff Lefton said, "He's dang near got that log-house finished. You know, he never wasted a log nor hardly missed a day—except once."

They all knew what that meant; the day Holmes had buried Joe Mesa. They smoked and loafed and sneaked a look over at Brigham now and then. Since the day of

38

Mesa's burial no one had ever once mentioned retribution for the slaying of their former comrade.

Brigham knew how their thoughts were running, but he also knew something else—where his father had gone—so he carefully made his cigarette with a wooden face, lit up and exhaled as he looked from face to face.

"No one ever got hurt by what they didn't know," he said quietly. "Forget Russ Holmes, and as long as I'm boss don't any of you ride down there. He's got eyes like an eagle an' Tocannon Ranch can't afford to lose any more men. With Joe gone and Martin out of it that leaves just four of us counting my Paw—and without him only three."

The others said nothing. They looked out over the reddening range or they carefully studied the toes of their boots but they said nothing until Cliff Lefton swung half around towards Brigham with a puzzled expression and spoke out.

"I been on the Tocannon five years, Brig, but I don't expect I want to stay where the outfit don't stand up for its men. Suppose I'm down on the south range and come onto a Tocannon critter down there in trouble."

"You go help it," said Brigham, looking straight at Cliff.

"Yeah? Even if it's inside Holmes' boundary lines?"

"He's a stockman," responded Brigham. "He wouldn't make any trouble under those circumstances. You know that, Cliff; you said yourself he seemed like a regular enough feller."

"Sure. That was before he killed Joe. And I been thinkin' about that too, Brigham. Joe an' me was like pardners. We made the drives together, pardnered up on the winter feedin'."

Brigham kept gazing straight over at Cliff and began

39

to shake his head back and forth. Cliff stopped speaking and frowned.

"You're not all fired up to ride down there and shoot him, Cliff. You're tryin' to convince yourself that's the right thing to do, but you don't really believe it is. Or at least you're having trouble making yourself believe it is." Brigham flung away his smoke, looked over towards the house and looked back again. His expression was saturnine. "I can't make myself believe that's the right thing to do either, because of the way Joe snuck down there with his knife. If Holmes had done that killing differently I expect I'd rid down there with you. But he didn't, Cliff. He didn't."

Lefton turned his perplexed face away and flicked dirt off one boot. He continued to scowl though, and he looked to the others as though Brigham hadn't settled anything for him.

Brigham gazed over where a saddled horse drowsed patiently at the barn hitchrack. "Who forgot to unsaddle?" he quietly asked. One of the cowboys said he had. Brigham looked reprovingly at the man and instructed him to go take care of his animal, but as the rider stood up to obey Petl struck the triangle calling them to supper and Brigham said for the cowboy to care for the horse after they'd eaten.

They got up and started over across the yard. Around them there was a peacefulness, a hush, and a pleasant springtime warmth that had no breath of air stirring in it, which meant that summer was going to come early this year with its steady heat and its drying brightness.

They passed on into the house after washing at the out-back basin near the stirrup-pump, and they ate their supper saying very little, and as always, they passed back outside to have their final daytime smoke, and it was then that the man who'd forgotten to put away his animal said in soft puzzlement, "Hey; what become of my horse?"

They all went out a few steps and stared down through the settling dusk. The horse was gone.

"He busted loose," someone muttered, but the cowboy who had tied him there indignantly denied that this could have happened, so they all went walking on towards the barn intrigued by a minor mystery.

It was Cliff Lefton who inadvertently solved the thing for them. He stepped up onto the bunkhouse porch to peek in on Martin Crabb, then flung around and yelled to the others: "He's gone; Martin's gone! He ain't in his bunk!"

# CHAPTER SIX

THEY TRACKED MARTIN ON THAT SADDLED HORSE westward for a mile before the shadows, made increasingly darker as they got closer to the forested slopes, blotted out the sign. Then they sat for a moment discussing what must be done.

"Out of his head," said Brigham. "I wondered if maybe the laudanum wasn't wearing off when he got tossing about an hour or two back."

"But Miss Petl give him more of the stuff," put in Cliff Lefton worriedly. "Hell; he'll fall off out here somewhere an' if the bump doesn't finish him lying exposed all night sure should do it."

Brigham could make out the anxious expressions. They all knew how huge that westward forested country was, how trackless and remote. A delirious man on a horse he wasn't capable of guiding, could be anywhere

41

back in there. If it would have done any good Brigham would have sworn, but instead he said, "Split up and ride west, and if you find him fire two shots fast, let a minute go past, then fire two more shots. One thing; that horse has been under saddle all day. He'll stop in the first meadow he comes to and eat."

He looked at them and they looked back. None of their faces showed much hope. There was a thin-edged moon rising behind them and the sky was swiftly purpling. Brigham turned and rode off south-westerly. He didn't turn to see how the others would go.

He rode for a solid hour up and down, in and out. He tested the forest's stale fragrance for a faint scent of dust or horse-sweat, never caught any such smells and made for the little nearby meadows in among the giant trees. He knew all of this country well, had been hunting in it since boyhood. And he also knew the way of horses. But combining these talents brought him nothing.

Once, lower down and skirting zig-zag back and forth he thought he heard a horse running downcountry, but when he got clear of the forest-fringe to hear better, the rider was either out of hearing or it had been some trick of the night.

It was close to midnight before it occurred to Brigham that Crabb hadn't fallen off or someone would have found his grazing animal by now. He stopped, sat a while in solemn thought, then ticked off the places back in here Crabb might have got to. The trouble with this rational kind of reasoning was that he wasn't considering the acts of a rational man. Crabb had been out of his mind when he'd got up, staggered outside, saw that horse standing there and had gone over to climb upon its back out of life-long habit.

He reasoned that it was this same instinctive life-long

habit which had kept Crabb from falling off somewhere. Evidently, as long as Martin's instincts worked, he would somehow manage to stay in the saddle. The problem was, then, Brigham told himself, just how long could a delirious man remain conscious? He had no answer to that one; he'd never been around a man with a fractured skull before.

He urged his horse onward, bearing now southward through the forest-fringe towards Tocannon Creek, which was beyond Holmes' place, and which possessed a number of lush little meadows along its west to east course. He had covered all the other places that horse might have carted his delirious passenger, and these places would be his last hope.

Riding through patches of ragged starshine, he kept hoping to hear the spaced signal-shots, but they never came. He was a half-mile uphill and saw how moon-glow fell upon Holmes' walled-in log-house, glistened over his new-laid shake roof, and was surprised when he was half-way along to catch sight of an orange glow coming from a rear window. A man who worked hard physically all day long as Holmes had been doing ever since he'd come onto the Tocannon range, ordinarily dropped into bed at sundown and slept until morning like a dead man.

It didn't occur to Brigham that there might be good reason for Holmes to still be awake until he heard the opening and closing of a door, and after that the solid sound shod horses made walking over packed earth.

Brigham paused half up his side-hill gazing outward and downward. It was difficult to make anything out down there even though every sound carried well enough, so he dropped down a hundred yards and had an excellent sighting. But by then there was nothing to see.

He heard a horse squeal in that round corral, saw two horses fling their heads around at a third animal. The third beast lashed with her tail and whipped her head back and forth as a mare would do, and that was interesting to Brigham because he distinctly recalled studying Holmes' horses when he'd been down here before, and they were horses, not mares.

There was a fourth animal too, but this one remained saddled and tied to the rack in front of Holmes' house. Brigham sat and pondered. Curiosity rose up to dominate his thoughts. He knew there had only been one man at this place when he and his father had ridden over here. He didn't believe Holmes could have made any friends in the valley, certainly not among the other ranchers or riders, but perhaps what troubled him most was this nocturnal meeting. Who were those other two in there with Holmes; what were the three of them planning in the late night, and how had they come here?

He decided to find out, dismounted, walked back and forth in the forest-fringe until satisfied the onward route was safe, then he stepped out into the soft light, hesitated a moment and afterwards headed straight on over to the house.

It wasn't his intention to eavesdrop or try to peek in a window. He strode on around the south end of the place, cut to the left, raised a powerful fist and struck the front door with a blow that made the walls rattle. Inside, someone pushed back a chair. Brigham heard that raw scraping. He also heard what seemed like a swift, low exchange of words. He raised his hand to strike again and the door swung inward, Petl filled the opening looking very soberly up at him.

He stood with that hand still upraised, taken entirely unawares. She pointed past him where lamplight fell outwards over that saddled animal at the hitchrack. He turned, recognized her animal, and turned back again. She stepped aside motioning for him to enter. He did, and stopped just inside the door. Martin Crabb was over there stretched out his full length upon a long home-made slab-table and working over Martin with his back to Brigham was the squatter, Russ Holmes. He dropped his head to look around as Petl came up close. In a low whisper he asked some obvious questions. She answered him in the same soft way.

"I heard you out in the yard at home, Brigham. I heard the men say Martin had ridden away, so I joined the hunt as soon as I could, but since you'd all headed westward I decided to ride southward. I didn't find him, at least I found his horse down here but didn't see him until Mister Holmes took me inside. Since then we've been working to keep Martin alive."

Brigham's steady dark gaze ran over to Russ Holmes' back and lingered there. "Can he help, Petl; how bad off is Martin after takin' all that jolting?"

"He seems better than he did at home, Brig. Of course, he's unconscious now while Mister Holmes operates, but before that he was . . ."

*"Operates!"*

Petl put a hand upon her brother's arm. She re-provingly shook her head at him. "Be quiet; he said I could stay and help only if I kept quiet."

"He's operating on Martin?"

Petl nodded, looked stoically ahead and looked back again. "He told me that dented-in place behind Martin's ear was pressing against the brain and as long as it re-mained like that Martin might never regain full con-sciousness again, or he might not be right in the head. So, he's forcing that piece of dented skull back out

45

again, taking off the pressure and removing most of the cause of Martin's pain."

"How?" said Brigham. "Is he a doctor?"

Petl shrugged. "He didn't say. I didn't ask him." She looked up, her gaze unwavering. "But I'll put my trust in him, Brig."

For a while Brigham considered walking on over and watching Holmes at work. He instead turned abruptly on his heel, walked out of the house, swung right and walked out a goodly distance northward; went almost a mile out before he halted, drew his six-gun, fired two quick shots, counted fifty then fired two more.

After that he stood out there clearing his pistol cylinder of spent casings and replacing them with fresh loads from his shell-belt. When that was completed he hiked back down to Russ Holmes' yard and halted at the corral to study those horses in there. Later, he got the horse his sister had ridden and off-saddled, off-bridled the beast, hobbled it and turned it loose.

These things took time. He heard riders coming out of the north-westward night and stepped clear of all buildings to sight them. Cliff Lefton was the first one up. Cliff was anxious and drawn from his search. He asked Brigham several rapid questions, shooting them at him like bullets, as the others also rode on up. Brigham explained as best he could but he could no more answer the obvious questions than Petl had been able to.

The others dismounted and would have gone on up to the house but Brigham growled for them to remain outside with him. They stood out there feeling the initial chill of early morning, sometimes talking, sometimes smoking, always worried and constantly troubled.

"I once heard of this feller," said Cliff gloomily, "who loved to cut folks up. He didn't know nothin' about

46

doctorin', you see, but he had this urge to slash . . ."

"Shut up," growled Brigham. "Even if he didn't know what he was doing in there, it'd be better'n letting Martin lie around until he shrivelled up and turned into some kind of an idiot."

Petl came to the doorway and looked out at them. Cliff's mouth dropped open. "You didn't tell me *she* was in there," he said accusingly to Brigham. Brigham said nothing. He was somberly watching his sister. She beckoned to them. When they came softly up she moved slightly aside and pointed to a still form lying across the room on that slab-table with a bandaged head.

"How is he?" Brigham asked, swinging his gaze to the wide-shouldered, lean-flanked other man in that room where he was washing his hands and forearms in a basin of hot pinkish water. "Will he make it, Sis?"

Petl also regarded Russ Holmes where he was sluicing off. She said, "Maybe, maybe not. Mister Holmes said this should have been done for him the day after his injury. He says by keeping Martin doped and quiet we've lowered his resistance. If he has the heart of a bull he'll make it. If not . . ." She shrugged.

Cliff started to take a long step inside. Petl halted him with a scowl. "Not tonight. Maybe tomorrow. You go on back now. There's nothing you can do here anyway."

She closed the door against them and in a twinkling they were back in the total darkness again. Brigham looked at the others. "What can a man do when someone's skull is caved in?" he asked. "How do you get inside to push it back out?"

Cliff dolorously wagged his head. "You see him lyin' there? He looked dead already. Probably was." Cliff caught his breath, turned this over and over in his mind then faced the closed door. "We ought to go in there and

47

make danged sure he *ain't* dead."

"An' what if he is?" a cowboy mumbled. "Then what, Cliff?"

Brigham watched the uncertainty in Lefton's face. He said, "Do like Petl said—head on back for the home place, boys."

"All right. You coming?"

"No. I'll hang around and come back with Petl."

"Might be a long wait, Brig."

"Well. It's dang near dawn anyway."

The others left and Brigham went out by that round corral upended someone's saddle, sat down upon it and started building a smoke. What did you say to an enemy who had just saved someone's life? He lit up, tilted his head to blow a streamer at the heavens and afterwards dropped his face towards that log-house over there.

That same man had killed Joe Mesa. Did you avenge that or did you decide that one of these deeds cancelled-out the other one?

He smoked and wondered what his father would say in a situation like this. He flung down the cigarette and savagely ground it underfoot. His father wasn't here, wouldn't be back for another two days at the very least, and after suffocating all these years under a paternalism which was overpowering, now he had a decision to make all by himself.

And he couldn't make it.

He sat out there waiting for Petl scarcely conscious of the passage of time, scarcely aware of anything at all in his surroundings, engulfed in an agony of self-doubt. No matter how he decided, in old Stuart's eyes he was sure his decision would not be the right one. He already knew what old Stuart had had in his heart when he'd ridden off towards Winchester Pass. When he returned,

48

the fact that Holmes had saved Martin Crabb's life wouldn't change anything at all. Old Stuart had made *his* decision—the squatter was to die.

Brigham sprang up, planted his powerful legs wide and threw a fierce and bold look over towards the cabin. All right; he'd made his decision too—the squatter was *not* to die. Joe Mesa had come in the night as an assassin; he'd taken his chance with all the odds on his side, and he'd lost. There was no law which said men had to avenge assassins. But there *was* an unwritten law that recognized that when another man was a saviour of one's friends, one did not stand by and see that saviour gunned down.

He considered how it would be between himself and old Stuart when his father got back to the valley, and for the first time in his life, Brigham thrilled to the prospect of opposing the one man in this world whose word had been law for as long as Brigham could remember, and whose undeniable capability had been robbing his son of the right to stand on his own two legs for a long time.

# CHAPTER SEVEN

RUSS HOLMES TOLD PETL TO CALL HER BROTHER INTO the house and while she was outside he set about starting breakfast.

There was a soft blush lying over the valley now, it had been a long night, Russ felt drained as much perhaps from lack of rest as from the nerve-wracking thing he had done upon that Tocannon cowboy.

He hadn't known Martin Crabb but he'd heard his horse out in the night, and he'd got around behind Crabb as he'd also got around behind Joe Mesa. But the

49

difference had been surprising to him, for Crabb had been sitting his saddle like a drunk man. He'd offered no resistance when Russ had taken him down, had carried him bodily into the cabin, but afterwards he'd become violent. That was when the girl had shown up. He'd never seen her before either; hadn't known that old Stuart Campbell had a daughter, in fact.

Then, with the beautiful girl's aid, he'd done what had to be done. As he'd afterwards wearily explained to Petl Campbell, he wasn't a doctor but during the war he'd been a medical aidman and had assisted in many operations such as the one he'd performed on Crabb. The difference was that during the war there had been instruments and a place to work. Here, he'd had to improvise every inch of the way.

He also explained this to Brigham when Petl brought him back to the house, showed him the waxen, seemingly lifeless face of Martin Crabb. "If I hadn't," he said to Brigham, "your rider would have died. Not right away. Maybe not for a couple of weeks or longer."

Brigham gazed solemnly up at the lanky squatter after making his long study of Martin. "What're his chances now?" he asked.

Holmes shrugged. "I don't know. I'd say a little less than even. It depends on his stamina."

"How did you do it?"

Russ sat down on a bench. "Whittled a hole in the center of the pushed-in piece of skull. Put a steel pin from a spur rowel with wire around it through the hole, straightened out the pin inside, behind the bone, then made a sort of tourniquet-handle on the outside and slowly twisted until the skull was forced back where it should've been." Russ looked up at Brigham and wearily smiled, his eyes tired and dry looking. "Sounds simple, doesn't it?" he asked.

But Brigham, who knew nothing of healing at all, shook his head. "Doesn't sound very simple to me," he exclaimed, then turned half-around as his sister came forward and handed Brigham a plate and a cup of steaming coffee.

Brigham ate and drank—and thought. Petl and Russ Holmes exchanged an occasional word but Brigham ignored both of them until the sunlight came, striking out along the flat edge of the world, splintering into a million prisms.

It was this arrival of full day that made him stir, made him look out and around and see how much time he'd spent down here. He put aside his plate, his coffee cup, and stood up. He said to his sister: "You tell him about this land yet?" She shook his head without answering so Brigham looked straight at Russ Holmes.

"When my paw and I rode over here—even before that—I wasn't sure that you didn't have a right here. Not the kind of right my paw spoke of though, which was simply the right of being here first and holding the range against all-comers. I figured you might have *legal* right."

Russ stood up, passed over to take Petl's empty plate and cup and walk on past as far as the washpan where he left them, turned, and with his wide shoulders dark against the log-wall's peeled brightness, put a steady gaze over at Brigham.

"What you're getting at, I think," he said, "is that you're convinced I don't have any right to this land."

"That's right."

"Prove it!"

At the brittleness of that challenge Petl also stood up. She looked from one of these big men to the other. "My brother is right, Mister Holmes. Until yesterday neither he nor I were convinced you didn't have the right to squat. But we found an old Ute treaty made by my father and Red Kettle which gave my father his ten square miles of valley land."

Holmes stood gazing at Petl, and his gaze softened. He didn't say anything for a while. He walked on over to the fireplace, flung a stick in, walked back and gazed at Martin Crabb. Finally he turned and gazed at the Campbells. He said, "Listen to me, you two, I don't question the existence of that treaty, but the reason Tocannon range is shown on the homestead maps as being unclaimed is because there has never been any official title to the land granted to your paw or anyone else. If he kept that old treaty stuffed in a drawer some place, then how would the federal title examiners know it exists?"

Petl grasped this before Brigham did. "You mean if my father doesn't get this treaty approved as being in existence, he can't get title to the Tocannon Ranch?"

"That's exactly what I mean, and Petl, if I were you folks I wouldn't waste a whole lot of time taking care of that either, because when I was up there in Denver filing my claim, that was a big office and it was chock-full of other fellers also looking for land to file on."

Brigham went to a bench and dropped down. He suddenly seemed far less anxious to leave this place than he'd seemed not ten minutes earlier. He stared up at Holmes with his dark brows coming closer and closer together. Eventually he said, "One question: What happens to your claim if we get that old treaty recognized giving us legal title to Tocannon Ranch?"

Russ smiled wryly, "Why then I reckon you'll have a summer home and a winter home." His smile faded, he held up both hands and gazed at the blisters. "I'll chalk it up to experience and ride on."

Brigham began wagging his head. His stare brightened towards Holmes. "No, I don't think so," he muttered. "Because I think you knew the minute you told us to go file that treaty that the minute we did that, it put you out. That's what you were deciding about when you walked over there and looked at Martin a minute ago, and when you tossed that limb on the fire. You were makin' up your mind whether to do the right thing or the wrong thing."

"Hell," growled Russ, looking slightly unpleasant. "Don't try to make me out something I'm not, Brigham. Your paw won this country, it's his an' he's got a title I'd recognize as being plenty good. But you see, I didn't know there was any such a treaty when I came over Winchester Pass, or you can bet a good horse I'd never have worked as hard as I have these past weeks."

"He'll pay you for the improvements, Russ."

But the tall, blue-eyed range-rider shook his head at this offer. "Naw. Why should he pay me? I had no right puttin' him in a spot where he might feel obligated." Russ put up a hand, scratched his head and went after another cup of java. As he was pouring he dryly said, "You know, Brigham, I sure never had your paw figured as a man who'd be willing to pay a man for an honest mistake."

Brigham looked at Petl and she looked right back at him. He fidgeted a little upon his bench. "*I'm* saying Tocannon Ranch'll pay you."

Russ came slowly around. As he walked over, handed Petl a cup, walked over and handed another one to Brigham he nodded. "All right; *you're* makin' the offer then, and not old Stuart. The answer is still—no. Forget

53

it." He smiled. "It was good exercise anyway." He got the third cup of coffee, tilted it and drank. Afterwards he put the cup aside and said once more, "But your troubles have only just started, Brigham, if you don't get that treaty up to Denver, recognized and recorded. It's a mite early yet, but by mid-summer there'll be squatters in here thicker'n fleas on a dog's back."

Petl said, "Where will you go?" to Russ.

He shrugged and smiled. "I was riding when I came here, ma'am, and I'll be riding when I leave. I just thought it was about time for me to settle somewhere, to put down roots." He shrugged again. "But if Tocannon Valley's not to be the place, then I'll ride along until I find the right place."

Petl paced slowly over to the door, her face grave and her eyes thoughtfully downcast. Over there, she put down her coffee cup and gazed at Brigham. It was quite obvious what tangent her thoughts were upon now: Stuart. Their father's mission in the settlements. But all she said was, "I think we'd better be heading home, Brigham. The men will wonder if anything happened."

Her brother stood up, nodded, and shot Russ Holmes a long, solemn look, then he turned without a word and passed on out of the house. "Wait," he said to Petl. "I'll rig out your horse and fetch it back up here."

She waited. She stood over there in the open doorway with good morning sunlight and warmth coming in, watching Russ Holmes. He also stood gazing at her, and because he was a strong man with healthy urges, he greatly admired what he saw.

He went around picking up their empty cups and taking them over to the washpan. "Don't you think I'd make someone a good wife?" he asked her, then laughed as she smiled up at him.

He paced over to the doorway, stood beside her looking out where the world lay soft-lighted and ideally warm. "Quite a valley. I saw it the first time about four years back." He dropped his eyes to her face. "I don't blame your paw for being willing to fight to keep it unspoilt."

She returned his gaze without moving, without dropping her face nor even lowering her gaze. He was, in her eyes, very handsome, very much a man, and there seemed to be something about him which was different from other men, even when he smiled down into her eyes as he was doing now.

"But you know, Miss Petl, I had no idea until about midnight last night just how doggoned much beauty there was in this valley."

She didn't smile back at him. She thought he was poking fun at her, trying to embarrass her with this rough compliment. But it was not always possible to understand exactly what men really meant, which she knew, so she did not smile, she simply turned and stepped on through into the yonder sunlight where she halted.

"You may be killed," she said simply to him, looking northward towards the hulking shoulders of Winchester Pass. "My father, after you talked to him yesterday, rode home disliking you very much. He has never been a man who overlooked things."

"Yeah, I know," he replied, looking northward over towards the corral where Brigham was fitting up the horse Martin Crabb had ridden down here, with a squaw-bridle to lead the animal away with. "He's a tough old devil, Petl. I know his kind. That's why I put it on the line for him. Only, I made a bad mistake. I didn't know about the Ute deed. Well," he smiled at her again. "I'll apologize  the next time I see him. Anyway, when I pull out he'll have his land back—with some improvements which he may—or may not—be able to use. I don't figure he'll be too wrathy—will he, Petl?"

"Yes," she answered candidly. "He is wrathful right now. He left yesterday for the settlements."

"Oh?" His blue gaze lost a little of its warmth and had a questioning intensity to it as he watched her lovely face.

"He told my brother he was going for a doctor and for some medicines. My father does not lie."

Russ was gazing at Petl's profile. He now raised an arm, put it outwards against the cabin front wall and leaned there upon it watching her profile carefully. After a little while he said, "I think I see what you're not quite telling me, Petl."

She raised her soft, dark gaze to him, waiting. With her, as with her brother, there was a powerful heritage of intense loyalty from both sides. She would not speak openly in opposition to old Stuart, and yet she could not allow this handsome big man who had saved Martin Crabb's life and who had also shown the Campbells how to save their Tocannon empire, to be shot down by some hired assassin.

"He didn't ride to the settlements just for medicines and a doctor, did he?"

She still said nothing. But neither did she look away from him, and at this juncture in their quiet conversation Brigham walked up leading three horses. He stopped, looked from his sister to Russ Holmes, got a swift, shadowy expression that passed instantly, and wordlessly held out the reins to her horse.

As she moved over beside her animal and swung up, she looked straight downward at Russ and shook her head.

56

Brigham also got astride. He moved heavily, as though he were tired. But that didn't seem to be all that was bothering him. "We'll look in on Martin from time to time," he muttered without looking at Russ. "If there's anything you need down here, or anything we can do—just name it."

He pulled his direct, blue gaze off the beautiful girl and put it upon her brother. "Just pray," he murmured. "I think about everything's been done that can be done. The rest of it is up to Martin—and Providence."

They thanked him again, turned and started slowly on out of the yard. He stood there watching them for a long time. He ran a hand over his scratchy jaw, finally, turned and walked back inside, his thoughts making his steps drag, making his tiredness more pronounced. Sometimes a man finds himself in a position that isn't easy to define. The girl was strikingly lovely; she'd seemed—but perhaps it was only his imagination—to be receptive, to be interested in him.

And old Stuart's son was different too from what he'd seemed the day before when he'd come down here in his father's company.

He crossed over when Martin Crabb moaned, studied the gravely ill man for a moment, then went to the fireplace and started to make a pot of broth from venison. Being busy sometimes aided a man in making decisions, in coming to the *right* decisions.

If that old devil of a Stuart Campbell had gone out of the valley to hire himself a gunman, Russ felt he was capable of taking care of that. But what bothered him now was fighting that old iron man. He had no wish to kill Stuart. In fact, even before he'd talked to Brigham and had seen Petl, he'd felt no compulsion along those lines. But now, after knowing the beautiful girl, he

57

recognized the utter irreconcilability of such a course, for whether those two thought their father was wrong or not, they would be loyal to him. He worked over the broth for Martin Crabb and pondered his peculiar position.

# CHAPTER EIGHT

CRABB SEEMED TO RALLY WITHIN MINUTES AFTER RUSS got some of the venison broth down him. He remained unconscious, at least delirious, but he seemed stronger and much less lethargic. After a while even his pointless mumblings began to have continuity to them.

Russ cleaned up, shaved, cared for his animals and went outside for a smoke. He considered his well-located corrals, his nearly completed log-house, even the start he'd made at digging a well close by. He'd amply wet this ground with his perspiration but he was a man with his share of philosophical fatalism too, so he could view all this, knowing now that it would not be his after all, without turning vicious or bitter about it.

He was aware too of the elemental fact that if he wished to file a legal protest against Tocannon Ranch, wished to fight old Stuart's unrecorded early-day deed to this land, there was an excellent chance that he could win.

But there were other considerations which, to a man of honor and ethics, left him believing a person who would start his new life by making mortal enemies of his closest neighbors over something they had overlooked, or had been innocently unaware of, was hardly the way to start creating a new, fresh life.

He did not refuse to recognize that Petl had

58

something to do with this decision. Earlier, when both she and Brigham had been there and he'd first learnt that such an old-time deed to the range really existed, he'd had to make his decision, and he'd made it conscious of her liquid soft gaze upon him all the while.

He finished the smoke, killed it, got up and made some thoughtful calculations. Petl had said her father had left Tocannon Ranch the day before, which meant old Stuart, heading for the settlements beyond Winchester Pass, would have struck out from home early and would have ridden steadily all day yesterday, perhaps late last night, and would have come to the first town some time after midnight last night—perhaps about the same time Russ was puzzling over that delirious cowboy reeling in the saddle out in his gloomy yard.

Assuming old Stuart had made good time, by this time today he would have purchased what supplies he needed, would also have probably tried to hire a medical man to ride back into the valley with him—and would also have located one of the brotherhood of gunfighters which haunted the settlements always ready and willing to ply their vocation for an advance in cash.

He looked far northward where Winchester Pass's heavy shoulders rose starkly up against the soft-saffron morning sky. Old Stuart might bring his killer back with him, or he might send him on ahead, but in either case the gunfighter would have to come down through that pass up there. There was another road into, and out of, Tocannon Valley, but it was about twenty-five miles southward and for Stuart Campbell's purpose would be useless.

Russ went inside, took his holstered six-gun out, emptied it upon the table and sat down to meticulously clean and oil the gun. He afterwards did the same with his carbine. He could do no more than that, unless it was anticipate old Stuart, and this too he moved out to do by saddling one of his horses and leading it over to the cabin while he ducked inside to get his carbine. When he emerged he spotted a horseman coming towards him from the east where the golden sun struck hard, brilliant lights off the rider's accoutrements.

He waited there by his front-door hitchrack until he knew who that man was, then he thumbed back his hat and let Cliff Lefton come right on up.

Cliff tipped his head in somber greeting. "Was down this way," he said, eyeing Russ thoughtfully, "and thought I'd stop by an' see was there anything I could do for Martin."

"There is something you can do," said Russ. "Get down and I'll show you."

Cliff swung down, strolled over, looped his reins at the rack and followed Russ on into the cabin. Over beside Crabb's improvised bed Russ said, "Stay here and watch him for a while."

Cliff looked around. "You got to leave?"

Russ nodded. He was bending over making a close inspection of the massive bandage upon Crabb's head. As he straightened up and saw Cliff's expression, he said softly, "You object to watching your friend, Cliff? Everyone else's done a heap more than you have, so far."

Lefton scowled, stung by this. "I don't object at all. Only Brigham sent me down here to watch for springin' heifers and if I don't show up at the ranch he's goin'. . ."

"I'll tell him where you are, Cliff. I'm goin' right by Tocannon Ranch."

Lefton's expression turned crafty and speculative.

60

"Right past it," he murmured. "There's nothin' but more Tocannon range past the home place all the way on up to the mountains."

Russ didn't elaborate. He put a caustic gaze upon Cliff for trying to draw him out, picked up his hat where he'd tossed it, and turned away. Over at the door he said, looking past Cliff at Martin Crabb, "He probably won't need any watching, but he was mumbling a while back and moving his arms a little. If he fell to the floor now, it could very easily kill him. Just pull up a chair and make yourself at home. If you get hungry there's venison broth in that pot by the fireplace."

Cliff looked unsettled by all this. He viewed Martin Crabb askance. Once before when Martin had begun to deliriously fling his arms around Cliff had almost stampeded. As Russ passed on out of sight Cliff called after him.

"Hey! Don't you forget to tell 'em at the home place where I am. An' tell 'em to send someone down here to spell me off too. I'm not very good at this kind of stuff."

Russ didn't reply but as he stepped up over leather, reined around and struck out northward, he was gently smiling down around the mouth.

There was a slow build-up of heat over near the westward hills but out a mile upon the range it was still benign in the early daylight. He passed several bands of grazing Tocannon Ranch cattle, eyed them with a range-rider's quick and sharp interest, and passed them by.

It was a long ride from the southerly places on up to old Stuart Campbell's main ranch, but as Russ went along he compared the miles he had to traverse with the miles old Stuart had yet to cover before he was even close to Winchester Pass, and he felt no need for urgency.

61

Tocannon Ranch's weathered, mighty buildings showed up across the gold-lighted horizon a little short of noon. Russ, coming on in from the south was not detected right away, but the first man to finally notice him sang out letting everyone else know a rider was approaching.

Brigham hadn't sent the riders out today, excepting young Cliff, but they seemed to Russ to wish that he had, for no self-respecting horseman ever enjoyed cleaning greeny watering troughs or patching broken corral stringers, it was vastly beneath their dignity. Still, these too were the requisites of cow ranching, so while they showed in their strained, disapproving faces that none of this menial work would ever meet with their favor, they'd nevertheless do it.

When Russ rode into the yard though, everyone paused at whatever he was doing to turn and watch as Brigham and the lanky squatter came together out in the dazzling brightness.

Russ explained about Cliff Lefton. Brigham listened and nodded. "Sure," he said, "one of us'll go down after a while and spell him off. You figure to be gone very long?"

Russ didn't say, he only shrugged. How did you tell a man you were going up into a Pass, pick a nice big boulder to get behind, and waylay his father? You didn't, so Russ let his shrug say all on that score he'd volunteer.

"The thing is, Martin's got to be kept still. If he gets to flinging around he could undo all the good with one hard bump."

"I understand," said Brigham, making a slow, thoughtful survey of those obviously freshly-cleaned and oiled guns.

"Maybe your sister could go down," suggested Russ. "She seemed to have a way with her around the ill."

"Yeah, she has," agreed Brigham, drifting his black eyes from Holmes' guns back up to the lanky man's rugged, frank and forthright face. "I'll ask her. She'll probably be glad to."

Russ nodded, looked over at the main house, caught no sight of Petl over there, looked around the clean, big yard, showed the rangeman's approval of kept-up buildings, and lifted his rein-hand. "See you later," he murmured, dropping Brigham a light nod, and rode on northward out of the yard.

Brigham stood a long time without moving, his expressionless dark face watching the lanky man's departure. Then he slowly turned and made a slow, seemingly reluctant, dragging call at the two cowboys on across the yard.

"You fellers saddle up. Rig out my horse too. I got something to say to Petl then I'll meet you at the barn an' we'll head out."

"After him?" one of the riders asked.

Brigham gave this man a dark, wintry look, turned on his heel and walked over towards the house.

Petl was in the kitchen when her brother walked in. She listened to everything he had to say and made no comment until just before Brigham walked back out again. Then she said, "What are you going to do if he really is bound for the Pass?"

And Brigham turned to show her a dark and deter- mined expression. "Keep 'em apart is about all I can do," he replied. "You got any ideas?"

"Just one. Try to get to paw before he comes down the south slope."

But Brigham had evidently already considered this

63

for he now wagged his head at her. "It wouldn't do any good. You know paw. He's got his mind made up."

"Brigham; paw's always had his mind made up. Ever since we were children he's had his stubborn beliefs."

"I know that," said Brigham dryly. "Maybe I even know that better'n you do."

"Well; is it *always* going to be that way? Do you and I have to stifle our own feelings all our lives because they don't happen to be the same as his?"

Brigham came back into the room from the doorway. He stood big and solid and hard-muscled, gazing over at his sister. "No," he quietly said. "Not always. I'm crowding twenty-five this year, Petl. That's time to take a stand now and then. It's been a long time comin' but it's here—the day I stop keeping quiet about things I disagree with."

She smiled. "Then stop him before he gets down the south slope, Brig. Don't let him send some gunman-killer, some settlement riff-raff, to kill Russ Holmes."

Brigham gently inclined his head. "That all it means to you?" he softly asked. "You just don't want Holmes killed, Petl?"

"No. There's more. He saved Martin, didn't he?"

"Maybe. We won't know for some days yet whether he saved him or not."

"And he could've shot you and paw yesterday, couldn't he have?"

Brigham shrugged. "Perhaps. He looks fast with guns—but paw nor I are the slowest." He shifted his stance, raked Petl with a long look, then said, "What else, Sis; come on—what else is it?"

She saw his expression and understood it; these two had come to maturity together, they understood one another perfectly.

64

"I don't know," she said. "I'm—not sure, Brig." Then she faced fully around towards him. "Would it be wrong?"

He stood stolidly unmoving for a while thinking upon this unspoken thing which was there in the room with them, and because he was not a man who spoke rashly nor came to decisions without a lot of thought, he did not reply until almost a full minute had passed.

"No, it wouldn't be wrong. You're twenty-two, Sis. 'Be twenty-three this coming Fall. I'd say it was high time you came around to this." He turned, went back to the door, pushed it partially open and looked over his shoulder at her. "I think it might be the best thing that could happen around here, and besides that he's the kind of a man other men cotton to."

Brigham walked on out, slowed near the corner of the house to lift his hat, resettle it atop his heavy black mane of hair, and stroll on towards the barn where those two cowboys were waiting with three saddled horses. As he walked he tried to imagine his sister married; married to anyone for that matter, not just to Russ Holmes. He couldn't quite get around such a bizarre notion. For one thing, who would do the cooking?

He got across to the others, took up a set of reins, mounted without a word and led the way northward out of Tocannon's yard. His companions exchanged a knowing look; Brigham was riding over the trail of Holmes, heading in the identical direction.

# CHAPTER NINE

WINCHESTER PASS LAY SOFT-LIGHTED IN AFTERNOON haze long before Russ Holmes got near its low-down foothills with their shade trees and underbrush. Higher up, where the slopes and forested rims stood stark against a faded sky, there was a quiet darkness, a purple shadiness. But where the old road itself wound around, climbing steadily, there was a lighter shade to the day, because up in here most of the roadside trees had long ago been cut down and grimly burned so that no ambushes could be brought off.

As Russ made his study of all this he thought it probably had been old Stuart Campbell himself who, after one ambush in the days before the wagon-ruts were up here, had set about having those ambush-sites eliminated.

It was a very good guess. It *had* been old Stuart who had nearly lost his life there in the early days and had made bleakly certain no such occurrence would ever happen again.

There were other indications of that directing genius in the Pass as Russ passed higher. For one thing, where a little seepage spring came out of a mountainside and had previously lain stagnant and inaccessible, straining hands had rocked out some enormous stones, dug a channel, and had laboriously made a passageway for that run-off water to fall into a pool beside the road where horses could be watered.

Russ saw these things and could not help but admire the vision, the foresight, the perseverance of old Stuart Campbell. How could it be that some men had the

66

genius and the pioneering knack, while at the same time they also totally lacked the perception which would have allowed them to make the transmission safely from one era to another?

He had no answer for this, but he strongly suspected that pioneers, like artisans, had the ability only to create something. Then others had to come along and sustain it because in the restless soul of pioneers there was not and never had been, very much patience for the endless details of regulated existence.

He got half-way up the Pass before he saw what he sought; a mammoth boulder shaken loose in ages gone from the overhead crest which had tumbled into a little fold in the mountainside where it had rested ever since. This, he smilingly thought, was the one ambushing spot old Stuart could not change. It commanded a fine view of the lower-down foothills, of the great, hazy width and length of Tocannon Valley, and it also commanded an excellent view of the roadway, which lay east of it and perhaps a hundred feet lower down a gentle grassy incline.

Russ pushed his horse on up to that huge boulder and dismounted while he explored this place. He found evidence that he was not the first person ever to pause around behind that gigantic stone; there was a rotting little stack of carefully-placed firewood, and a few feet from that was the frontiersman's oven—a stone-ring made around an ancient collection of black char.

Recalling the faint outlines he'd see earlier where some old-timer had once had a shack, he considered it highly probable that this same long-departed old scout or trapper or whatever he had been, had used this boulder for his hideout too.

When he was satisfied, Russ mounted up and went

poking on westward along the broad mountainside. There were grassy little depressions up in here showing plenty of game signs, and there were also barely discernible old skid-trails where men with teams had cut logs, barked them, and chained them to double-trees for the skidding of them down to the valley floor. He thought he could guess who had done that, too, for every building on the Tocannon outfit had been made out of this same kind of a big stalwart pine or fir tree. He didn't see any other riders coming up into the Pass because he was busily exploring this new country westward. Once, when his horse seemed to have caught same familiar scent down their back-trail and attempted to turn, to nicker, Russ had growled and the animal had turned obediently to going along with no more outbreaks.

He was satisfied, an hour later, and started back for the boulder. He considered it very likely that he would have a night to himself up here, that Stuart Campbell and whomever he brought back with him would not arrive in the vicinity of Winchester Pass until the following day, probably around noon. Still, as long as Brigham Campbell had agreed to care for Martin Crabb down at his homestead, he felt no urgency anyway, and since he was reconciled to abandoning his claim he actually felt, as he off-saddled by the big boulder and hobbled his horse, relieved of all that planning and responsibility.

And yet a man feels regret at coming full circle; not because of the sweat wasted but because of a dream destroyed. As men advance along through life their dreams become more vulnerable but none the less cherished. Russ thought he would not give up *this* dream; if it was not meant to happen here, it would

68

happen for him somewhere else.

With that small consoling reflection he settled himself to watch day's ending, then an odd thing happened. Somewhere over against the darkening hillside north of him a horse whistled, making a sound which carried a long way. He became instantly alert without moving. He hopefully thought this might be a Tocannon Ranch remuda grazing up here; a number of horses which were not needed and had been turned loose.

But a horseman's instincts are rarely deluding. Seldom do grazing horses in familiar country become separated or lost, and the call of that animal, in Russ Holmes' experienced opinion, was the sound of an animal unfamiliar with his surroundings and in earnest quest of companionship.

He got up, faded out around his boulder, went down where his own animal was and watched the reaction here. His horse was standing motionless looking straight up the slope and westerly in the direction of that sound, which was what Russ had wanted to verify for himself. He thought he knew where that noise had come from but in a matter such as this he preferred trusting another horse.

He returned for his carbine then went zig-zagging on up the westerly hillside in search of that strange horse. Trees and underbrush made it possible for him to move with small chance of detection and by the time he'd cautiously got a half-mile uphill there were also deepening shadows to aid him.

He didn't find the horse but he found something which interested him much more; a camp with three men in it. He first saw them from over the lip of a bony ridge. They were down below where salt-grass grew near a seepage waterhole. They had pack outfits

69

scattered around among their saddles and guns, and for as long as he lay up there watching the three of them did nothing. They had evidently come over the top of Winchester Pass about the same time Russ had been coming up-country, but for some reason he did not entirely understand, those three had swung westerly across the sidehill instead of taking the easier and more direct route down into Tocannon Valley.

He thought this a suspicious thing for riders to do—unless they wished not to be detected entering the valley.

The three men were sitting in their littered camp talking idly. Smoke rose up from cigarettes and while it was not possible to make out their faces, Russ could see enough to realize that these were range-riders of some kind. They were spare, lean men, armed and attired in well-worn boots, hats, and butternut shirts. Their levis were faded and shiny from much wear. They could have been common cowboys except for those pack outfits. Cowboys passing through a country rarely had pack-horses along.

*Settlers!*

The idea struck him like a blow. These men were doing the same thing he had done! They were land claimants.

He drew back a little, sat up and thought about this. It occurred to him too that these strangers had been careful where he had not; they had asked in one of the settlements about conditions in the Tocannon country, had evidently been warned against old Stuart's resolve to hold his land against all-comers, and had decided not to risk an encounter with Campbell or his men, and had therefore followed Winchester Pass only to its top, before angling away from the possibility of detection.

He eased forward for another long study of those three. One of them was gathering twigs for their supper fire now. Another one was ambling off through the trees evidently to go check their animals. The third one stood up and mightily stretched, yawned, and said something to the man making the fire which brought back a short, gruff laugh.

Then Russ stiffened where he lay. Passing up-country towards those men, evidently also drawn to this spot by the inadvertent call of that uneasy horse, were three other men. These newcomers were moving slowly, very carefully, keeping trees and underbrush between them and the camp until, less than forty feet away, they halted to also make a study of the strangers.

Russ recognized Brigham Campbell at once by his size and his darkness. As he lay watching it dawned upon him that the Tocannon men had been following *him*. There was no other explanation for them being up here like this.

Brigham stepped noiselessly forth and approached within fifteen feet of the camp before that yawning, stretching man saw him. At once this man became motionless and stiff. From the corner of his mouth he said something. Russ saw the other man, the one at the fire, slowly stand up and turn around, his right hand dropping low.

Brigham's voice was pitched low but it carried to Russ's overhead place in the abrupt hard silence. Brigham said, "Howdy; heard one of your horses nicker and thought I'd see if it was maybe one of our animals."

Neither of the two strangers said a word. They stood there eyeing Brigham carefully, their hatbrim-shaded faces invisible to Russ but their ways of standing spoke volumes. They were skeptical and wary and ready for

71

whatever came next.

Brigham moved on up and looked around at the pack outfits, at the carelessly flung-down tangle of saddles, bridles and blankets. He lifted his head only when a man stepped in from behind him and said, "Keep your hand away from that gun, mister."

This was the third stranger, the one who had previously walked out into the trees. He had his .45 out and aimed. Russ saw Brigham's head drop a little for as long as it took the dusky, big man to sardonically consider that drawn gun. Then Brigham raised his eyes and said, "Put it away, mister," in a tone so soft Russ scarcely made out the words.

"Sure," said the cowboy. "As soon as you explain who you are and what you're doin' slippin' up on folks like this."

"Well," Brigham replied conversationally, "to start with my name is Campbell. In the second place I didn't slip up on you exactly; I heard a horse trumpet and came up to see what was wrong. And finally, mister, if you don't put that gun up you'll get buried here."

Brigham turned his head down-country and nodded. The two riders with him came forward, both with their drawn guns covering that stranger.

When Brigham saw that the strangers had seen, he said sardonically, "Now put it up!"

The stranger obeyed, holstering his six-gun with a sudden gesture of veiled defiance. He said, "We heard about you Campbells; folks warned us we'd run into you."

Brigham gazed at the men and scratched the tip of his nose. "Did they tell you the folks at Tocannon Ranch eat strangers or something like that?" He made a gesture at the littered camp. "Why didn't you stay on the regular road, it would have saved you a lot of hard riding and there are much better camp-sites down in the valley."

One of the strangers, the man who had been making the little fire, hooked his thumbs in his belt, shifted his stance and put a considering gaze upon Brigham. "Mister Campbell," he said quietly, "what folks said was that Stuart Campbell claimed ten miles of Tocannon Valley and he'd run off Indians, bandits, and settlers, to keep it."

"Stuart is my father," stated Brigham. "I guess the rest of what they told you is correct enough. Is there somethin' wrong with a man fightin' to keep what's his?"

"No," drawled that rough-looking, unshaven rangeman. "Not if it's done legal-like. But at the land office up in Denver they made a title-search for us and determined that didn't no one named Campbell—or anyone else for that matter—have a recorded title to even one mile of Tocannon Valley, let along ten miles of it."

Brigham kept looking at this man. He was older than his companions and seemed to be their spokesman. Brigham wagged his head back and forth. "There's a deed to this land. It's not recorded yet because my father overlooked that. You see, he's been here fifty years and until right recently there's never been any question of land titles. But this was a Ute deed, and as soon as we can we're going to file it with the land office for recording—or whatever they do with land titles."

The strangers looked at one another. Brigham's attitude was not truculent, which counted in his favor. He was not vehement or threatening, and his words, quietly spoken, carried conviction. One of the other strangers scowled, saying, "Well; I told you fellers this was too good to be true—too easy."

73

The older man faced Brigham again. "Would you mind showin' us that deed?" he asked.

Most men would have bristled and Russ waited for Brigham to do that. But he didn't. He said, "Wouldn't mind at all. It's down at the ranch. If you boys'd care to rig up we can be down there before it gets plumb dark." He stood waiting. The strangers looked at one another. That older man removed his hat, vigorously scratched his head, dropped the hat back on and gave a big shrug.

"Hell of a note," he grumbled. "We sure had a long ride for nothing." Then his tone brightened. "Mister Campbell; you know of any other decent unclaimed land hereabouts?"

Brigham shook his head. "Not in Tocannon Valley. But on south down in the open country there's a thousand miles of unclaimed land."

"Any good?" one of the others asked skeptically.

"Some of it's good land, yes. The trick is to locate water first. Good water, not just seasonal runoff. In Utah unless you get year-round water you can't make it." Brigham looked at the strangers. "Want my men an' me to help you rig up for the ride down to the ranch?"

The strangers mumbled dissent saying they'd spend the night where they were and perhaps ride on down in the morning. Brigham accepted this, nodded and walked back down through the trees the way he'd come. His two cowboys followed after him and Russ, lying up there, listened briefly as the three disgruntled strangers spoke disgustedly back and forth.

The older man said he was satisfied without seeing that Ute deed. He also said the only thing that would be accomplished if the three of them wasted a day going to Tocannon Ranch to see that cussed paper, would be that they'd lose time on the trail. Then he said something

74

that alarmed Russ. He said: "You recollect all them other fellers takin' out claims on the land down here; well, if we don't keep on pushing along like we been doing, we'll maybe lose our lead and the others'll get down the plains beyond Tocannon Valley ahead of us."

Russ didn't wait to hear the replies of the other two men. He shoved back off his vantage lip, scuttled down through the trees the way he'd come, but instead of returning to his boulder he swung off southward moving fast in the hope he'd intercept Brigham and his riders before they were lost to him in the settling dusk.

He was sure Brigham had heard that horse whistle from the vicinity of the roadway leading up the Pass, so he angled downwards and easterly towards the trail, and he was correct. Long before he saw them he heard their shod horses.

# CHAPTER TEN

BRIGHAM WAS EVIDENTLY ENGROSSED WITH HIS personal thoughts because he didn't appear to hear Russ coming even though Holmes made no attempt to be quiet. When that burnt-off grassy right-of-way was reached beyond which there was no cover, and Russ stepped out into this, one of the Tocannon cowboys saw him and grunted in surprise. It was this grunt which brought Brigham out of his reflections. He also saw Russ and although he was in the act of mounting, he removed his left boot from the stirrup, dropped one split rein across his mount's neck, held the other rein in his hand and softly scowled.

Russ walked on up, halted and returned Brigham's long look. "You left too soon," he said. "You should've

75

hung around up there and listened to what those ridge-runners had to say after you left them alone."

Brigham's scowl deepened. "Where were you?" he bluntly demanded.

"On that knife-edged rim overlooking their camp. I heard that horse too."

Brigham looked at his cowboys. One of them was impishly grinning as though the thought of a white man out-Indianing a half-breed Ute amused him immensely.

"I told you and old Stuart a couple of days ago, Brigham. I said there would be more settlers come in here. Some this year, more next year, and still more in the years ahead."

"You did," agreed Brigham.

"But instead of listening, old Stuart went out to hire himself a gunman."

"That was his decision, not mine."

Russ said, "Yeah. He made his wrong decision and instead of using his head and riding for the nearest land office to have that old Ute deed recorded, he went off on some notion of bloody revenge—and left his Tocannon Ranch wide open for the squatters to gobble up piecemeal."

"You're not tell me anything I don't know," said Brigham coldly.

"Then I'll tell you something you *ought* to know," said Russ. "Stuart's gone and you're the boss at Tocannon now. It's what you say that goes. It's your decisions that count now. Never mind following me around or slipping into squatter-camps, Brigham. Take your fastest horse, put that damned Ute deed in your pocket, and light out for the county seat and have that damned deed recognized by a judge and recorded!"

Brigham's black gaze turned gradually bright as the

validity of what he'd just been told struck through him with its sound logic.

"Because if you don't," went on Russ, "and if that old fool of a father of yours keeps on trying to win everything with guns and fury—you're going to not only wind up an orphan, you're also going to wind up owning not one lousy acre of land. Sooner or later, Brigham, some of these settlers won't be our kind of men—like those three back up the mountainside—they're going to be land sharks who'll kill and burn to destroy that old Ute deed. And if that thing is ever destroyed . . ." Russ paused and slowly shook his head. "There are no Utes left around to swear there ever was such a deed, and without it being recorded, your paw can swear to high heaven it existed—and the bunch of you'll still lose your land."

One of the Tocannon cowboys brought forth a tobacco sack and went to work manufacturing a cigarette. The other man stood watching Russ with his forehead corrugated in thought. Brigham also seemed to be concentrating upon all that had just been told him. Finally he said, "Hell, Russ; I can't head out for the county seat. Not with paw headin' back this way with a hired killer. Someone's got to be here to . . ."

"You damned fool," exclaimed Russ in great disgust. "What's more important—some two-bit gunslinger—or Tocannon Ranch?"

"That's not the point. The point is that if he kills you—if you and paw get into . . ."

"Listen, Brigham; there's no other way. You only have two men left—and your sister."

"*Petl!*" exclaimed Brigham. "*She* could take the deed into the . . ."

"A girl—alone—making a ride like that?" Russ said a

77

coarse word. "You listen to me, Brigham. I wouldn't let you do that to her even if she volunteered. But even if I would, you'd have to send at least one man along with her—*and you can't spare another man!* Get this through your skull. That deed's got to be recorded within the next four or five days—otherwise the squatters will be flocking in here and without any visible proof you own Tocannon, they'll resist being thrown off—which simply means your paw's gunman'll be working night and day. We don't want that to happen, because right or wrong, the first time your paw resorts to murder, the law'll be after him. *You* take that deed to the county seat. We can afford losing *one* man for a few days because there's no other choice. But we can afford to lose *only* one man. And Brigham—if I were in your boots I'd get atop that damned horse right now, right this minute, and I'd hightail it for home, change horses, get that deed, and turn right around and head for the county seat—tonight!"

Brigham nodded. He'd already made up his mind to do these things. But as he turned to step up over leather he said, "How about you, Russ?"

"Two things you can do for me, Brigham. One; tell these men here that until you get back they take orders from me and no one else—not your paw or any gunfighter he fetches back with him. And the other thing—tell Petl to change off with Cliff on keeping watch over Martin until I get back down to my place."

Brigham turned his horse, gazed at the two cowboys and said nothing at all, only lifted his eyebrows at them. First one rider nodded, then the other one nodded. Brigham said to them, "You've heard everything so you know what's right and what isn't right. When I get back I'll settle things with my paw."

78

"If you can," murmured one of those riders dryly.

Brigham shrugged, showing a sudden fierce defiance. "Whether I can or not, when I get back I'll head for Russ's homestead and we'll be four to one. I think my father'll find odds like that pretty hard to buck—even for him."

Brigham reined around and booted out his horse southward down the gloomy trail back into Tocannon Valley. One of those cowboys, gazing down the night after him, softly said, "I sure hope you're right, Brig, for your sake as well as my own sake. But that old man of yours—he's a mountain lion of a man if I ever saw one." The cowboy turned and looked somberly from his companion on over to lanky Russ Holmes. He gloomily wagged his head. "I know how Brig feels, Mister Holmes," he said. "I reckon most of us as have been around Tocannon Ranch any length o' time have seen how old Stuart stifled him—but this—well, this is going up against the old man the worst possible way, and I can tell you for a solid fact that when someone bucks Stuart Campbell head-on, they ain't got too good a chance of walkin' away afterwards."

Russ listened and let this man have his say. He didn't offer any argument although the Lord knew there was plenty to be offered in rebuttal. All he said was, "Let's get on up where I left my outfit. I'll saddle up and we'll drift on up closer to the top-out. Before I had reinforcements, and before it occurred to me that old Stuart might get cute and try cuttin' westerly like those strangers did, I figured to stop him about even with that big boulder where I hobbled my horse."

"You," one of the cowboys said, "figured to stop old Stuart?"

"Just long enough to disarm his imported gunfighter

and send him back the way he came, is all."

Russ turned and started legging it up the northward road. Behind him the Tocannon men gazed at one another, on up where Russ was fading out in night-gloom, then they got astride and walked their horses along behind him until, with that mighty old boulder showing soft-lighted and ghostly on the left, Russ told the range-riders to wait. He went alone on up where he'd left his outfit, caught his animal, took it back to the rock, rigged out and got astride. He then returned to the waiting cowboys and without saying a word motioned for them to follow along as he turned uphill again and rode steadily towards that higher-up pale slot where Winchester Pass's eroded eminence bulked dark against a paler sky.

When the three of them were high enough to see far out below them, down across the endless wastes, one of the riders said, "You figure on waitin' up here until old Stuart shows up?"

Russ, understanding how this man's thoughts were running, replied without directly answering that inquiry. "If we let Campbell get by, then there's going to be trouble. If we kill the night up here and as much of tomorrow as it takes, we can do the job a lot easier—with any luck."

"Yeah," murmured the second rider. "With a *lot* of luck." This man was briefly quiet, then he said in a resigned way, "Stuart'll fire us for this."

"Will he fire his own son too?" challenged Ross.

And the cowboy answered without any hesitation. "I think he will, yes. You don't know old Stuart. You had one run-in with him. Me, I been a Tocannon rider nearly five years. I hired on the same summer Cliff Lefton did. If I've learnt anythin' about that old devil in those five

80

years it's that when he says somethin' you better do it, and when he don't like something—look out."

Russ looked over at this man, marveling that Stuart Campbell could inspire such solid respect in a man as he'd obviously inspired in this one. It was very close to dread, in Russ's eyes.

He dismounted, hobbled his horse, tugged off the saddle, removed the bridle and stood back while his hobble-wise animal crow-hopped off the road and over to the first stiff-standing clumps of bunch grass.

The Tocannon men followed Russ's example, and afterwards the three of them killed time in idle conversation and thoughtful speculation. A little before midnight with a chill little breeze whistling up the northward canyon from that black, raw run of uninhabited onward land, they heard a rider passing up towards them from the valley side.

Russ got up and sauntered down to intercept this man, knowing it would be Brigham. It was, and he saw Russ long before he ordinarily would have because he was expecting to be intercepted.

As Brigham reined up he patted his coat. "I got it," he said. "By tomorrow afternoon unless there's some hitch, I'll be at the county seat havin' it recorded." Brigham dropped his hand as those Tocannon cowboys came forth through the night. He watched their doleful faces a moment then made one of his rare small smiles.

"You two look like you've just signed up for a lost cause. Don't worry too much; if my paw fires you I'll re-hire you."

"The trouble with that," pointedly said one of those men, "is that your paw'll fire us all over again." Then this cowboy made a little shrug and a little tough smile. "But I reckon we was lookin' for work when we come

81

to the Tocannon so we'll be lookin' for it again when we leave."

Brigham said to Russ: "Petl wasn't at the home place but Cliff was. I told him what I was doing. He said I was crazy to go up against my father."

"Was Petl down with Martin?" asked Russ.

"Yes. Cliff said before he left down there he and Petl got more of that venison stew down him and he seemed a lot better." Brigham shook his head. "I always figured when a feller got operated on he was sure to die." He lifted his reins, gazed at Russ a moment longer, then nodded gravely and eased on by. "Be careful," he said. "See you day after tomorrow."

They watched him pass across the little level stretch of ground, tip downwards and begin the dusty descent to that northward inky world far below.

"Good man," one of the cowboys said, his words soft, his intonation firm. "Russ; I think you done something for him. Right or wrong, I think you give him somethin' he's needed a long time—a shove in the right direction."

This man went over to a stump, sank down there and started making a smoke. "The Injuns used to sit up on these consarned hilltops all night waitin' for visions. All I ever get from this kind of monkey business is the chills and maybe a sore neck or back." He lit up, doused the match, deeply inhaled, exhaled, and composed himself for the interminable vigil with that peculiar philosophical resignation which all old cowboys had, and which was, uniquely enough, almost identical to the same lasting patience the Indians had also possessed.

The hours wore along. Russ bedded down where a swale protected him from the chilling little wind, and slept. The Tocannon men visited for a long while after Brigham had gone down towards the yonder plain, and after Russ had gone to sleep. They discussed many things, but they began their conversation and ended it upon the same topic: Stuart Campbell.

"It ain't just gettin' fired," one of them said. "It's havin' to face the old devil like this."

"Yeah. An' him with some bloody-hand bronco gunfighter along with him. I got a feelin' the smartest thing for us to do is put one man down there in the road to halt 'em, and have the other fellers back in the brush with carbines."

This suggestion found acceptance with the listening cowboy, so he nodded over it. "And the natural man to walk out there and halt 'em in the roadway, is Holmes. He worked this whole thing up. It's his idea."

"Yeah. Tell me—what'll happen if Brig an' the old man meet down there, come morning?"

"Naw, they won't meet. Old Stuart'll be sleepin' in his soogans when Brig rides right on by."

"But the old man's goin' to raise hell an' prop it up when he finds out what's going on—where Brig went."

"Yeah; I used to envy Brig, havin' a paw who owns half Tocannon Valley. Not tonight though, and not until I see how his buckin' the old man works out. Might be I'll be glad just to be me, after all."

Russ's voice came out to those two sternly. "Roll up in your saddle-blankets you two, and shut up," he said. "It's bad enough sleepin' up here so's I can help someone beat me out of my homestead, but bein' kept awake all night by you two is just too damned much. Now shut up and bed down!"

The cowboys looked soulfully at one another, got up and walked off into the brush with their smelly saddle-blankets.

# CHAPTER ELEVEN

DAWN CAME WITH A SWIFT RUSH AS IT OFTENTIMES DID in the summertime mountains. The sun jumped up, flooded the world with dazzling light, and Russ Holmes went sleepily over to see the horses. They had by far had the best night of it because sound horses slept standing up and therefore had no aching backs and sore muscles from lying atop one thin old saddle blanket over rocks.

The Tocannon riders arose, scratched their bellies, spat, hawked and spat again, looked wetly down over the land below and looked at one another.

"Unbelievable," mumbled one of them, "what human beings'll do for thirty a month and meals, ain't it?"

The other rider didn't even answer, he just rubbed his eyes and afterwards watched Holmes return from seeing to their animals.

It took an hour of warming sunlight to bake all the aches and stiffness out of those three and by then hunger set in. None of them had any food along so they had a quiet smoke for breakfast then, one at a time, they killed time by walking on foot back down where that little run-off spring fell into its man-made pool at roadside, and there washed.

Russ had the mid-watch when he spotted riders approaching the north entrance of Winchester Pass. He passed along the word.

There were three men and the center one was recognizable to the Tocannon men. "That's old Stuart on his big black horse sure as shootin'," one of them affirmed. Then this man made another doleful head-wag and said, "Dang it all—the closer I get to a showdown the less I like this."

Russ, who had previously made his appraisal of old Stuart, concentrated upon studying the other two riders. One was a spare, whipcord man wearing a short jumper-jacket and a stiff-brimmed black hat. He had the easy posture in his saddle of a lifetime rider. This one, Russ thought, would be old Stuart's hired gunman.

The second rider was shorter, stockier, and rode as though he were obliged to do it, not as though he felt any kinship to the beast under him. This man also wore a narrow-brimmed nondescript grey hat and he seemed to be nearly as old as Stuart Campbell also was. Because this man carried no carbine under his rosadero and Russ could make out no hip-holster nor shell-belt, he thought this one must be the medical man Stuart had also gone to the settlements for.

Then Russ made an error; because he and his pair of Tocannon cowboys were atop their vantage point and seemingly had all the advantage, he grew relaxed and sardonic. If there was an excuse for his laxity it was due to the simple fact that his generation of men had come to maturity in the last days of the Western Conquest; in simple words this meant simply that Russ, never having had to feel peril in the shadows around him, was unaccustomed to the extreme caution and constant suspicion of the earlier environment which had molded and sustained men like Stuart Campbell. He sat up there watching those three small figures near the bottom of Winchester Pass, his carbine lying forgotten across his knees, totally unaware that the same sunlight which warmed his back and shoulders, also sent downward a hard, bright and metallic reflection for old Stuart's trained eyes to instantly see and correctly appraise for what it was.

"They're in the Pass," muttered one of the cowboys.

Russ nodded. "Be up here in maybe an hour or an hour and a half."

"How you figure to work it?"

Russ yawned, stretched his legs and put aside the carbine as he half-turned to cast a slow glance off to the right where the roadway lay. "You two can take places in the shadows and I'll stop 'em in the trail. You back my play."

"You reckon that gunfighter'll try an' make a fight out of it?"

Russ didn't think so and said as much. "If he sees your gun muzzles he'd be a fool to try it, and my experience with men like that is that they're not fools. At least not when they're lookin' into the business-end of a loaded gun."

The cowboys stepped over and looked downwards. Old Stuart and his companions were beginning the gradual descent. They were alternately in plain view, then lost to sight as they rode on around some jutting shoulder of land.

It took a long time, longer than Russ had thought, for the three of them to pass on up towards the top-out. Once it occurred to him that this delay seemed more than accidental so he sent one of the Tocannon men down the north slope a hundred yards where a cliff-face stood straight up, to lie down and keep watch. This man signaled with his hat that he'd seen the travelers, then he scrambled back up where his companions waited and reported that the riders were resting their horses down there; sitting there talking while their animals had a 'blow'.

Russ accepted this because it was normal procedure in mountainous country. It didn't occur to him that something was wrong until, a half-hour later, he distinctly heard only one horse coming on up the roadway.

He listened, looked at his companions, saw that their faces were reflecting sudden concern, and started down towards that cliff-top himself to have a look. He hadn't covered more than twenty yards when a hundred yards further down, and westward, a carbine exploded throwing up dust less than thirty feet from him.

He whipped around, sprinted back for the top-out and dropped flat where the Tocannon cowboys were already lying low and astonished looking in the scanty underbrush of their windy eminence.

"I'll be damned," one of those men said, sounding awed. "They must've seen us before they even got into the Pass."

Russ had already made this identical syllepsis, so all he said was, "Keep your heads down."

In the crushing silence following that solitary gunshot they distinctly heard that horse down on the trail still plodding along. Once, one of the Tocannon men muttered something and twisted as though to peek outward and downward. Russ ordered him to remain still.

"That'll be the stocky feller—the doctor," he said. "Old Stuart and the gunman are west of us comin' up towards the ridge. They deliberately sent the doctor on up so we'd be fooled."

"We were," dryly said a cowboy.

Russ inched ahead, parted some sage limbs and scanned the downhill slope. There was nothing moving that he could determine, and there wasn't a sound down there. He kept his vigil a long time because he knew Stuart and the gunman were somewhere along that downhill slope, but when this vigil proved fruitless he

87

crawled back to the range-riders, told them to watch the westerly rim, and slithered along until he was within sight of the roadway. There, he saw that short, stocky, older man coming straight along towards him, his worried face turning right and left with patent uneasiness as he came right on up to the top-out.

Russ rolled once, got both legs gathered under him and sprang down upon the trail. The doctor's horse snorted, rolled its eyes and came to a stiff-legged, jarring halt which threw its passenger hard against his saddle-swells.

The doctor straightened up and looked disapprovingly at lanky Russ Holmes. He said, "Young man; whatever you're up to let me warn you—Mister Campbell and a gunman he hired down in the settlements are going to flank you."

"Thanks for the information," said Russ dryly. "There's something Mister Campbell doesn't know yet. I'm not alone up here. But there's something you can tell me—are you a physician?"

"I am. Doctor Joseph Pecora. Mister Campbell told me he had a rider at his ranch with a fractured skull."

Russ shook his head. "His rider's not at Campbell's place, he's on down-country a few miles at my homestead."

"Ahh; I see. You moved him."

"No, Doctor. He was delirious, got on a saddled horse and rode down to my place in the night."

Doctor Pecora's eyes popped wide open. He stared straight at Russ.

"One more thing, Doctor, then you can head on down into the valley. I trepanned his skull."

"You—*what*?"

"Used a spur-rowel shank and a piece of stout wire to

88

pull his dented skull back off his brain."

The elderly medical man sat up there mouth agape. Finally he said, "Tell me, mister—whoever you are—just where did you learn that technique; are you by any chance a qualified medical practitioner?"

"Only an aidman during the war, Doctor. I've seen that operation performed a hundred times or more, and because I was convinced Campbell's rider was going to die unless someone did something—I tried it."

"And is this man still alive?"

"He was yesterday."

The elderly doctor crossed both his hands upon the saddlehorn and looked down his nose sternly at Russ. He seemed to be searching for words, but in the end all he did was shake his head.

Russ said: "Another question, Doctor. Did old Stuart say he meant to flank me up here?"

Pecora nodded, still keeping his thin lips pressed tightly together.

"And this gunman he has with him—do you know him?"

"No. All I know is what they said to one another on the ride up here. And if you happen to be Russell Holmes, let me tell you that between them they mean to kill you."

Russ's gaze turned ironic. "Glad you told me," he said. "What else did they discuss?"

"Nothing of any great importance. But if they had, Mister Holmes, you may rest assured I wouldn't repeat it to you."

Russ nodded at the old man. "You can ride on, Doctor," he said. "When you find Martin Crabb—the injured Tocannon cowboy—you'll find Stuart Campbell's daughter with him. Do me a favor—don't

89

tell her I'm in a fight with her father. It couldn't possibly help old Stuart and me, and it'd upset her."

Doctor Pecora stared hard at Russ. He seemed to be in the act of making some adjustments to some preconceived ideas. Finally he said, "Mister Holmes; why must you and Stuart Campbell fight?"

"Because he's forcing me to it, Doctor. I had in mind something different. That's why I'm up here now. I had in mind halting him before he could draw a gun, disarming his gunfighter, sending him back to the settlements, and telling Stuart there was nothing for us to fight about because I'm going to relinquish my homestead on Tocannon range."

The doctor tipped back his hat and looked puzzled. "On the ride up he told us you'd filed on his land, had built a cabin, and were making improvements." Pecora paused, put a close look upon Russ, then said, "Are you telling me now you propose to abandon all that?"

"That's right, Doctor. And that's what I'd hoped to have a chance to tell him before he cut loose on me with guns."

"Well," said the medical man looking off westerly along the ridges, "you shouldn't have sat up here with your carbine in your lap because he spotted the sunlight reflecting off it two miles out."

From this explanation Russ had his answer as to how he and the Tocannon cowboys had come under that sudden attack. Then the physician pursed his lips, rolled up his eyebrows and said, "But I think we can stop this right now, before someone gets hurt. I'll just ride on along that rim over there and hail them. They'll recognize me and listen, and we'll end it right here."

"You," said Russ a trifle roughly, "will keep right on riding down this trail into the valley, and on south until you see a new-made log-house over against the westerly hills. That's where your patient is waitin' for you, Doc, and that's where you're going."

"But, Mister Holmes, I'm the only one who knows both sides of this fight, and I could . . ."

"Get a gut full of lead, Doc. If there's one thing we *don't* need up here it's a wounded medical man. Now you go on and leave Stuart Campbell to me."

The physician sputtered another protest, so Russ stepped up to his horse's head, yanked some slack in the reins, started the horse on down the southern slope and gave it a light pat across the rump. As Doctor Pecora went on by he twisted to glance downward. Russ shook his head adamantly. "No arguments, just keep riding. And, Doctor—like I said—say nothing of this fight to old Stuart's daughter. Just tell her you saw me and I said I'd be back as soon as I could make it."

Pecora's horse, finding the downhill footing agreeable, picked up a little speed as he walked along, bearing his stocky, short and elderly passenger on down towards the valley floor.

Russ watched a while, then crawled back up the little grassy slope to the first sage clump, and after that he inched his way back over where the Tocannon cowboys were uneasily waiting.

One of them twisted to show a sweat-shiny face. "We seen movement over towards the west slope near the rim," he whispered.

Russ looked, saw nothing, and said, "Point out the spot."

Both the cowboys flung up their arms. Russ nodded, raised his carbine and levered off three rapid shots into a big buckbrush thicket. Limbs and leaves and dust exploded from the heart of that undergrowth, and somewhere beyond it and slightly further along the rim, a man's spurs or gunbarrel, or some other metal accoutrement struck rock and a harsh ring as that savage gunfire flushed a potential sniper.

Russ ceased firing, cocked his head to listen as someone over there retreated swiftly back down the north slope, then he plugged three more Winchester shells into his carbine and said to the cowboys, "Keep sharp watch. They're tryin' to get across this ridge and down the south slope to flank us. Don't let 'em get across this ridge whatever you do." He ran a long look out and around, then said, "This flanking business works both ways. So far, they think I'm alone up here; they won't expect *me* to try and get around behind *them,* and you boys are going to help me do that. After I leave here, every once in a while one of you toss a slug over there so they'll think I'm still up here on top. You understand?"

The Tocannon men nodded, but didn't look at all pleased about this, and Russ started crawling away.

# CHAPTER TWELVE

THE MORNING WARMTH INCREASED AND THE LAST OF that little gusty breeze that came up the northward slot of Winchester Pass died away.

As Russ crawled from cover to cover seeking his enemies the warmth piled up promising a hot day. He saw nothing, but then he hadn't expected to, and it was a tedious business, this creeping along lizard-like worrying that old Stuart or his hired killer might spot movement.

He found the place beyond the buckbrush clump

where a man had been lying near the ridge, and with his slitted gaze studying the onward ground he detected where roiled dust and skid marks indicated that flushed sniper had made his abrupt retreat.

By following out this mark he could see where the man had got down-country along the north slope as far as a stunted tree. There were several trees close to this spot and since these offered the best available protection it appeared very likely old Stuart and the gunfighter would still be close to them somewhere.

He started along parallel to those trees meaning to get well west of them before beginning his northward, flanking crawl, when one of the cowboys far back fired a shot in a ground-sluicing manner down the north slope.

Russ flattened, awaiting the reaction to this. For a moment there was none, then a six-gun roared, and it wasn't behind those trees after all, it was easterly, over towards the road, which clearly meant Stuart was still bent on his flanking tactic, only now he was attempting to accomplish it from the opposite direction.

Russ lay a moment debating, then he turned and started straight back where he'd left the Tocannon riders. Sweat ran into his eyes and ancient dust rose up in his face, but he got back and hissed at the cowboys to make certain they would not fire on him.

They were still huddled close and looking more than ever distressed. He wasted only a moment explaining, then went on past towards the road.

Here, there was about a fifteen-foot drop, and because he'd jumped down here before, when the physician had come along, he headed for the same drop-off. Once on the road though, while he was protected from an immediate sighting above by that very same shoulder of land, he was very much exposed otherwise.

He hurried along towards the Pass's cresting top-out, figuring that was where his enemies would also hit the road and he was right. He heard the man up above long before he saw him, jumped over to flatten against the high bank, and when a sailing silhouette in a short jumper-jacket and stiff-brimmed, low-crowned hat came leaping down, Russ was less than ten feet from the gunfighter.

He had his carbine swinging to bear. For a second before the stranger struck ground he swung his head and saw Russ. With agility no one could have expected, but obviously prompted by the gunfighter's instant realization of his desperate peril, the man twisted in mid-air and kicked outwards. His heel struck Russ's carbine under the barrel wrenching it half free of Russ's hold. Then the gunfighter lit lightly down on both feet cat-like and without a second's hesitation sprang inward.

Russ had to drop the carbine and whirl away to avoid the man's viciously arching six-gun. As this blow missed he whirled back, struck the gunfighter high up knocking him off balance, then ducked down and struck the man again lower down.

The stranger dropped his six-gun, doubled over to shield his middle, and sucked back. Russ went after him with his left hand pawing at the man, with his right hand drawn back and cocked to fire. But the gunfighter was no novice either and he'd already demonstrated his quickness and his agility. Russ's pawing left found only empty air. The gunman, disarmed now, got away, took in a big breath, eyed Russ from two close-set, vicious eyes, then danced in lashing out. He found Russ with two light but stinging jabs. He found him again with a

94

hail of little flurry-strikes. Emboldened then, the gunfighter whipped in closer, both fists working, and Russ was forced to turn sideways and take this punishment along the ribs until he could weather the storm and get set for a solid strike of his own.

He let go that cocked right fist and missed. He lunged and threw two powerful strikes, and missed again. He had the power but his adversary had the speed of lightning. He whipped backwards from Russ's blows and came bouncing back like a rubber ball to flick those hurting little jabs in and out, in and out.

Russ changed tactics. Instead of trying to catch this writhing snake of a man with lunges, he took a flat-footed stance and forced the gunfighter to come to him.

The gunman did come at him, but not in a rush as Russ had hoped, he came instead in a mincing way sometimes moving around Russ to the left, sometimes abruptly reversing himself and coming along Russ's right side. Always though, he kept that stinging little jab darting in and out.

Dust rose up scuffed to life in the trail by their moving feet. The sun beat down bringing a limp sweatiness to their clothing. The gunfighter's low-crowned black hat was lying in the roadway and the man's gun was near it. Russ still had his holstered six-gun but he neither had the time nor the inclination to use it now; this was man-to-man and while his .45 could have ended it quickly it would have been a shabby victory to triumph that way. He had no doubts though that had the circumstances been reversed old Stuart's hired killer would have used *his* gun, but this did not, in Russ's view, make it right for him to fight the same way, so he concentrated on turning, shifting, ducking and weaving as those little blanketing jabs kept lashing

95

out at him, awaiting the one good chance he needed.

He didn't get it for a long while; this settlement renegade was evidently not only experienced in the use of firearms, he was also a good man with his fists. If he'd had any power behind those strikes he'd have whipped Russ, possibly, but all he managed to do was sting him.

The man suddenly stepped back, dropped his arms, breathed deeply for a moment and said in a breath-gone way, "Come at it, cowboy; you couldn't beat your way out of a paper bag." Then he smiled and danced in again, confident of Russ's flat-footed solid stance, which was a mistake, because Russ had now accomplished what he'd hoped to achieve; the gunman was satisfied Russ could not move fast and would not push the battle. He flicked out a long jab and Russ launched himself low and hard straight at the gunfighter's middle.

In a frantic effort to escape those reaching fingers old Stuart's hireling gathered himself to spring clear. But he had no time to get set; Russ hit him with his right shoulder, got his hands upon the man's riders' short jumper, and held on with a power the other man could not counteract with all his wild writhings.

The gunfighter's expression of sweaty confidence vanished. He dropped his head and the pair of them glared, their faces less than a foot apart. He hammered at Russ's middle and tried chopping high, downward blows into Russ's unprotected face, but these were not well-directed blows and Russ, pushing his face against the man's chest, escaped most of them. He then locked his arms powerfully around the gunfighter's middle, set himself, and gradually constricted his arms lifting the gunfighter, who was as tall as Russ also was, six inches

96

off the ground in a mighty bear-hug.

The fight had been silent up to now except for the whip-saw breathing of the battlers. Now there came a high, keening bleat from the gunfighter as he kicked, threw himself backwards and forwards attempting to upset Russ, and hammered downward with his free fists.

His face began to turn splotchy pink. His mouth dropped open and his eyes bulged. Russ kept increasing the pressure squeezing every bit of air from his adversary's lungs. Those little raining blows grew wilder. They missed entirely and even when they connected there was no longer any force behind them.

Russ suddenly flung open his arms and jumped back. The gunman hit the ground, staggered, doubled over coughing and Russ waited until the man's purple face lifted, then he struck him with a sledging blow squarely between the eyes and the fight was over.

Where the gunman collapsed in a little burst of roadway grey dust his right hand, ironically enough, was touching his six-gun but the man was as unconscious as a stone.

Russ went over where his carbine lay, put both shoulders against the cool lift of roadside earth and leaned there gulping air. He didn't move for nearly a full five minutes. Not until one of the Tocannon cowboys came tumbling down off the overhead slope looking awed. He watched this cowboy walk out, poke the gunfighter with his carbine barrel, squint into the man's glazed eyes, stoop, pick up that six-gun lying there, and turn back.

"You all right?" he asked with enormous respect. "Mister Holmes; you hurt?"

Russ shook his head. It was becoming gradually easier to breathe again. "Where's old Stuart?" he asked.

The cowboy lifted his shoulders and let them fall. "We been watchin' like hawks but there's been no noise, no movement, anywhere down that side-hill. That's why I come down here."

"Why?"

"We figure he's either comin' along towards this road or else he's gone back to their horses to maybe head for the ranch and fetch back reinforcements."

"He's due for one hell of a disappointment if he heads for home," said Russ, pulling himself together, drawing himself upright off the cool claybank. "Go get your pardner," he ordered. "Fetch our horses down here. We'll head for the ranch too—and we'll take this carrion with us."

The cowboy looked uncertain about this suggestion but he started away with a little ragged wag of his head.

Russ went over, knelt beside his downed adversary, felt for a hide-out gun and found not one, but two little chrome-plated .41 derringers which he appropriated. He also found a wicked, long-bladed Mexican dagger in the man's right boot. This weapon he flung into the brush with a saturnine expression; one thing no one could ever accuse old Stuart of was an inability to hire genuine killers when he decided he wanted a man-hunter on Tocannon Ranch.

The cowboys came along with their horses, and obviously one had told the other what he'd seen happen down there in the roadway because the cowboy who hadn't seen the fight's ending was just as grimly impressed as his companion was when they halted where Russ was sharply slapping the gunman's face in an effort to bring him around.

It took almost five more minutes to get that beaten man to even focus his eyes, and even after he came

98

around he still could not stand erect without support for another couple of minutes.

Russ said to the gunfighter: "What was Stuart's plan?"

The gunman pressed both hands to his soft parts; he was clearly still in considerable pain from that bear-hugging. "If you're Russ Holmes," he croaked, "his plan was to see you dead an' buried."

"I don't mean that. I mean what was his plan after you two supposedly got me up here in the Pass?"

"To bury you up here and never say another word about it. Then go down where you built your shack and burn everything to the ground. He was in a hurry to get you socked away."

"I can imagine," said Russ dryly.

But the gunfighter weakly waggled his head. "No you can't," he muttered. Then he looked at the Tocannon men. "Either of you fellers got a canteen?" he asked.

Before the riders could answer negatively Russ said, "Why can't I imagine old Stuart was in a hurry to get rid of me, mister?"

"Water," repeated the gunfighter.

"Not until we get a mile down the trail," stated Russ. "Now answer my question."

"Because," croaked the gunman, "there was a big party of settlers in the settlement before we left, askin' questions about how to reach Tocannon Valley."

Russ stared at the man. So did his range-riding companions. It came to Russ now why old Stuart hadn't remained up here to conclude this fight after his hireling had disappeared eastward in his vain attempt to flank Russ.

"He figured to head for the ranch, round up his men, and come back up here to stop them?" Russ asked.

The gunman nodded as he carefully began to straighten up, his two hands still pressed to his middle. "He said if we didn't halt 'em up here an' they got down into the valley they'd scatter out and we'd have to hunt 'em down one at a time."

Russ motioned at the Tocannon men. "Get astride. One of you take this whelp up behind you. We've got to stop that old devil before he starts a *real* war."

They settled across leather with their hatless captive and Russ rode behind them on the downward trail leading southward back down into the valley.

He knew what old Stuart was going to discover when he got home—that Petl and Cliff Lefton were caring for Martin Crabb down at Russ's homestead, and that Brigham had ridden for the county seat to record that old Ute deed. But more than anything else, old Stuart was going to discover that his riders were no longer one hundred percent behind him, and this, Russ deduced, might inspire the old cowman to bellow like a bull and attempt to carry his war against the settlers in their camps single-handed.

Russ had no illusions about this if Stuart tried it. No matter how wary and experienced the old cattleman was; no matter how knowledgeable in the ways of night-time assaults and the Ute manner of firebrand warfare, he was still only one man and the settlers were many. He would be killed. Maybe not at first, but sooner or later the odds would lay him low.

"Damned old devil," growled Russ, unmindful of the looks he got from the others. "If he'd only hold off for two days there wouldn't be any need for any of this."

"How's that?" asked the gunfighter, interested.

"Shut up and ride along there," snarled Russ, cowing not only the gunfighter with his visible wrath, cowing

100

also those two cowboys along with him.

# CHAPTER THIRTEEN

THEY GOT TO THE TOCANNON HOME PLACE A LITTLE after high noon but old Stuart wasn't there. His big black horse was, though, and so was Cliff Lefton. Cliff walked out to meet them looking both puzzled and worried. In reply to Russ's first question Lefton said, with a gesture southward, "He come in here like a madman, rigged out a fresh horse, bawled at me to round up the boys and meet him down at your homestead. Then he dusted it out of here like a damned posse was after him."

Cliff looked at his two Tocannon friends and also at the battered, dishevelled prisoner they had with them. "Would somebody," he plaintively asked, "tell me just what the hell is goin' on around here?"

No one answered him right away. Russ swung down, went over and jerked his head at the gunfighter. As their prisoner slid down and flexed his legs Russ said to Cliff, "You got a good strong shed around here we can lock this feller into?"

Cliff's perplexed gaze deepened as he ran a slow look up and down the stranger. "I reckon the smokehouse'd do," he opined. "It's double-walled and . . . ."

"Yeah," interrupted one of old Stuart's other men as he also dismounted. "I never thought of that."

"Take him over there and lock him inside."

The gunman started a loud protest. Russ turned towards him with a cold stare and the man's voice trailed off into deep silence. Then he said, "Listen, Holmes; I still got half the money on me Campbell give

101

me down at the settlement. I'll just hand it over for you to give back to the old devil, then I'll head back where I come from."

"The trouble with that," said one of the cowboys, "is that if you didn't head back, mister, we'd have all this to do over again. And I just ain't a man who believes in pushin' his luck too much."

Russ caught the killer's sleeve and gave him a rough push forward. "Lock him up," he ordered. "And hurry up about it. We've still got some tall ridin' to do."

"What about a guard?" asked Cliff Lefton. "If he had a day or two I think he could gnaw his way out'n there."

Russ nodded and pointed to the cowboy who'd shown the least aggressiveness up at the Pass. "You stay here and keep watch," he said. "And you remember what Brig said—you're not takin' orders from old Stuart any longer."

The cowboy nodded, drew his six-gun and poked the gunfighter in the back with it. "March," he said. "Head for that greasy lookin' little house over yonder with the smoke stains on it." The gunfighter started moving, but he threw Russ a dark look as he did so.

Russ turned back towards Lefton. "Your friend here and I both need fresh horses," he said.

Cliff nodded. "All right," he assented. "But I figure I'd better head out of here with you, because if old Stuart comes back in the same frame of mind he was in a while back and finds I've let you have a Tocannon animal he'll carve a hole in my middle and jump his horse through it."

They went into the barn and off-saddled. Cliff brought another horse from an out-back corral and began rigging this animal out with his own saddle and bridle. As the three of them worked Russ explained in crisp sentences to Cliff what had so far transpired. Then he said, "We're going to take old Stuart by hook or by crook, because if we don't I've got a feeling he isn't going to hold back on hitting those damned settlers even if he has to try it by himself."

They rode out into the yard, finally, swung southward and put their mounts over into a long lope. For a mile they rode like this saying nothing, then Lefton called out a raw curse and pointed southward.

"Smoke!"

Russ spotted it at once even though it seemed to have only just commenced rising up in the still warm air.

"Your log-house," called forth the other Tocannon cowboy. "That doggoned old devil's went and fired your homestead."

Russ's expression was less concerned with his burning house than with what else old Stuart might have done down there. He called over to Cliff: "Are you sure Petl was with Martin at the house?"

Lefton nodded. "She hasn't come back an' I wasn't to ride down to relieve her until later. She'll be down there all right. Hey, Russ; you don't reckon Stuart'd fire the place with Martin lyin' in there, do you?"

Russ had no answer to this but he urged his horse out into a stronger run. The other two kept pace with him. For another mile they watched that smoke turn greyer and heavier as it was shot upwards by compelling tongues of pale flame.

When they finally saw the burning log-house Cliff let off a long string of blistering profanity. It was clear he was not especially concerned with the house either.

They came closer, finally, and met a head-on wall of fierce heat. Over near the forest where those westerly slopes began climbing upwards towards a purple height, someone ran out to wave at them with a white cloth. Russ veered off. His house was an inferno, his corral poles were cast down and neither of his other horses were anywhere in sight, but as he closed the gap between that short, burly figure over there frantically flagging them on in, he sighted two saddled animals tied back in some trees.

Cliff Lefton called inquiringly forward at the older, bareheaded, grizzled man who had waved at them. Russ recognized the doctor and told Cliff who he was. They slowed to a slamming trot and covered the last thousand yards at that gait, then Russ hit the ground before his animal had stopped, halting a few feet from Joseph Pecora.

The elderly physician's face was pale but his eyes were alive with a hard and bitter light. "Stuart Campbell did this," he said, pointing with a rigidly indignant arm towards the raging fire over at Russ's log-house. "He was like a bronco buck-Indian. He was entirely different from what he'd been on the ride back with us yesterday, Mister Holmes."

"Forget the house," said Russ, peering up into the shadowy forest. "Where's Petl?"

"Back in the trees with Martin Crabb. She's all right. She and her father had a terrible argument. When she refused to leave the house he fired it anyway."

"Where is he now?"

Doctor Pecora made a little fluttery gesture and shook his head. "He rode out just like he rode in—like a madman. I don't know where he went. I think . . ."

"Never mind," said Russ brusquely, starting on past towards the yonder forest. "How's Martin?"

Pecora turned to pace along with Russ and his pair of solemn-faced companions. "He's actually been rational,

104

Mister Holmes; it's the most amazing thing I've ever seen. Are you sure all the medical training you've had was only as a medical aidman during the war?"

Russ didn't reply. Petl came out to meet them, her expression showing deepest shock. She nodded without speaking and when Russ dropped his reins and started over where a hastily salvaged pallet lay, she turned back and went with him.

Martin Crabb gazed straight up at Russ, his eyes clear although his face was otherwise slightly blue and slightly puffy. He licked his lips and attempted a weak smile.

"She told me," he said to Russ. "She told me how you did it. I'm sure in your debt." Martin paused, looked slowly at Cliff and the other Tocannon man, and said in a thick, low-pitched voice, "Watch out for the old man. He's gone bronco."

Petl touched Russ and when he turned she moved off a little distance. When he followed and they were beyond earshot she looked gravely up at him. "How did you escape the hired killer?" she asked.

He shrugged that off as unimportant right then. "Caught up, disarmed him, took him to your home place and locked him in the smoke-house under guard. Where did your father go—back up to the Pass?"

"No. He didn't believe me when I said Brigham wouldn't ride with him in this. He said he'd go back and get our other men. He said he'd take them up to the Pass. But right now he'll be somewhere on the range looking for them if he doesn't find them at the ranch."

"He won't find them," said Russ. "There's only one man left at the ranch and he told Brigham he wouldn't obey your father. Maybe the old devil won't try it alone."

"He will," she said, watching his eyes. "You know he will."

"Yeah. Well, Petl, I'm going to take Cliff and head for the Pass. We've got to stop him. The other man I'll leave here with you."

"I won't need him now that the doctor is here. You'd better take him too."

Russ shook his head at her. "Just in case he comes back," he said. "Or in case Martin needs something from the ranch, I'll leave him here."

"When should Brigham get back?"

"Maybe tomorrow, if he makes good time."

"It'll be too late, Russ."

"No. Maybe not. If Cliff and I can catch old Stuart before he shoots a settler or two, it won't be too late."

"I wish Brigham was bringing the sheriff back with him," Petl said quietly, dropping her eyes. "It would be better to see paw under arrest for burning your house than seeing him dead in the dust or being hanged for murder."

Russ put forth a gentle hand, lay it lightly upon her and said, "If it's humanly possible Cliff and I will stop him before it comes to that."

"I hope you can," she murmured. "But I don't think you're his equal in the mountains."

Russ, thinking back to how old Stuart had caught that reflection of sunlight off a gun-barrel two miles from the Pass, privately agreed with this, but he didn't say so. He said, "What does the doctor think; will Martin make it?"

She nodded. "He'll make it." Then she averted her face and he saw a quick shadow pass across it as she said, "My father wouldn't even help us move him out of the house before he fired it. If the doctor hadn't been

106

here I don't think I could have got him out alone. I never saw my father like this before."

Russ gazed over where a great shower of sparks sprang up as his recently completed roof fell in amid a great cloud of smoke and raw noise. He said, "I think your mother's people have seen him like this, Petl. I think you're seeing him as he was twenty, thirty years back; more savage than any redman, more fierce and unrelenting than any warrior chieftain. If he awed you today imagine how he must have struck dread into the hearts of the Utes."

"So they gave him his ten square miles of land," she said quietly, and lifted her eyes to his face again. "Russ; it must have been terrible, living in those days."

He thought that it had indeed been terrible, but he also thought that to judge yesterday by today's standards was very wrong, so he said, "Times change, Petl, but men seldom change with them. Don't blame your father too much. He only knows one way to wage war."

"Like a savage, Russ."

"It's been a savage life for him."

"You're defending him. Look at your house. Look at what he tried to do to you with that hired killer."

Russ took her arm and started slowly back where the others were clustered around Martin Crabb. "The house was his anyway because I built it on land that belonged to him. He'd have burnt it sooner or later anyway, Petl. As for the rest—his hired gunfighter didn't earn his money, and your paw's not going to win at this other thing he's got in mind either—if I can help it."

"You should be his bitterest enemy, Russ. You shouldn't be trying to help him. Why are you?"

He halted, half-turned and said, "I don't know.

107

You're part of it. So is Brigham. And I reckon in another way I admire what your paw has been, and what he's faced with nothing but a gun and raw courage."

"And if he kills you . . . ?"

Russ made a little shrug. "My horse could fall with me and do that, Petl. Or I could catch a disease and die too."

"Or—if *you* kill *him* . . .?"

He turned and started on towards his horse again. This thought had occurred to him before. He said, "I won't kill him. If I have to wing him I will, but I won't kill him." He stopped beside his mount and looked down into her eyes. "I wouldn't ever want something like that between us. Do you understand?"

"I understand," she said.

He called over to Cliff ordering Lefton to get astride.

Petl said, "Russ; I'll be down here waiting. You will come back?"

He nodded at her, turned and stepped over leather. He and Cliff then loped away.

# CHAPTER FOURTEEN

THEY RODE HARD TO REACH THE FOOTHILLS OF Winchester Pass and Russ thought that if old Stuart had done as he'd said, had made a big sashay of Tocannon range seeking his men, he probably would be well behind them.

They found no fresh tracks which was reassuring, and as they rode past that little man-made pool of clear water half-way up through the shadowy hills Cliff Lefton loudly sighed in relief. They slowed and rode the last mile at a walk.

"Beat him," said Cliff grimly. "Now all we got to do is try an' ambush him."

Russ was about to comment on this when somewhere on ahead, over the top-out and down the far side, a man's strong bellow rang out.

Cliff looked bewildered until Russ reminded him of those settlers the gunman had told them about, then his face cleared and his expression turned curious, turned interested.

They breasted the last rise, hit level land which ran perhaps a quarter mile along before dipping on down the far side, and caught the unmistakable scent of sweating horses. Later, they heard the sharp ring of iron shoes striking raw stone and Russ halted up there keeping watch upon the furthest rim of level land. It was not a long vigil he kept; a large, bearded man wearing a checkered woollen shirt dark with sweat and a dusty old shapeless Stetson hat came slouching up over the north slope, saw Russ and Cliff sitting there in the roadway, and instantly dropped his right hand.

Behind this man came two laden pack-horses. Behind them were other laden animals, all breathing hard from the long climb, then more men. Russ counted five horsemen and seven pack-animals including two little seal-brown jack-mules with wise eyes and strong backs. He hadn't expected such a large party. Neither had Cliff Lefton, for he now said out of the corner of his mouth, "Too many, Russ, and whiskers there in the lead don't look like a man who's talked out of anything."

Russ, studying the checkered-shirted brawny leader of these settlers, got the same impression. He said, "Don't touch your gun."

When the bearded, rough-looking big brawny man was less than a hundred feet off he drew rein. Behind him all those straining pack-animals halted instantly, obviously glad for this respite. Behind them the other men reined around to come up abreast of their leader.

Russ spoke out giving his name and Cliff Lefton's name. He asked where the men were going and got back the answer he'd expected.

"Tocannon Valley, Mister Holmes," rumbled the bearded big man looking wary but also looking relieved for some reason. "We got patent-papers on land down there. We're settlers."

"The way I've been told," said Russ, "there's no free land in Tocannon Valley, mister . . ."

"Andrews. Moses Andrews, Mister Holmes, an' the way *we* heard it there's plenty of free land down there," said the bearded man, his dark eyes hardening against Russ. "We also heard there's an outfit down there that's sort of hoggin' things and they won't take kindly to us comin' in."

"Tocannon Ranch, Mister Andrews?"

"The same. I take it your ridin' for them."

"You take it wrong," said Russ. "I homesteaded down there too. Came in only a couple of weeks back. I even built a house down there. Then I found out the truth— that I'd squatted on deeded land."

"Is that so?" said Andrews, sounding suspicious and looking straight over at Russ. "Then maybe you can explain to us how come there ain't no record of that land bein' deeded?"

"Until yesterday no one ever bothered to record the Tocannon deed, Mister Andrews."

One of the other newcomers, a weasel-faced, wiry, slight-built man said, wearing a little crooked and crafty smile, "Maybe you ain't familiar with the law, Mister Holmes, but the first feller to file on land gets it."

110

Russ didn't know this, but he knew something which could ameliorate it. "Friend," he said to the weasel-faced man, "if you turned around right now and rode as hard as you could for the county seat to file your claim, you still couldn't get there in time to beat Brigham Campbell, who left last night to file the Tocannon deed."

This seemed to hold those five men momentarily speechless. Then weasel-face, still bleakly smiling over at Russ and Cliff Lefton, said, "That may be, boys, and then again maybe this old Stuart Campbell sent you up here to tell us that to turn us back."

Andrews and the others took heart again after they'd listened to their companion make this statement. They nodded and kept their close watch on Russ and Cliff.

Cliff said evenly: "Send someone on over to the county seat and find out whether that's true or not, and meanwhile the rest of you come on back down into the valley and wait."

This appeared to also make sense and as the five settlers considered it Russ said, "But I'd advise you not to camp on Tocannon Ranch land while you're waiting."

Now bearded and truculent Moses Andrews said in a rough tone of voice, "We've heard all about this old devil who thinks he runs the valley. As for campin' on his range—that don't worry us none. They say he's only got four riders, himself and his son. Well, boys, we cut our teeth on rifle barrels too, if it's a fight he wants."

"A fight," said Russ, speaking directly to Andrews, "is exactly what we're trying to prevent."

Andrews drew back his long lips to disclose large white teeth. "Don't do us no favors," he said, and mirthlessly chuckled. "We don't need 'em. Now if you

111

boys'll kindly get out'n the way we'll head on down and claim our land."

Russ saw the truculence firm up among those men at Andrews' words and tried once more to halt them. "Suppose you go down and camp on Tocannon range, Mister Andrews, and suppose there's a fight and you afterwards learn what we've been telling you is the gospel truth?"

Andrews rolled his powerful shoulders and his black eyes sparkled. "Well, then I reckon you can say we got a good scrap out of it anyway."

This kind of an answer left nothing further to be said. If Andrews was the kind of man who would provoke a fight simply to participate in one, there was slight chance anything else Russ or Cliff could say would deter him.

Russ looked at the other men. They all seemed in accord with Andrews in this, even the weasel-faced man, who did not look to Russ to be the kind of a man who would fight if he could figure some craftier way of achieving his ends.

"It won't be much satisfaction if some of you get killed," he said.

Andrews came right back with his answer to this, indicating they had discussed this before. He said, "Pardner, we don't figure to none of us get killed. But we can promise Stuart Campbell one thing—*he* damned well might get killed!"

"Do you think Campbell won this land from the Indians and has held it all his life against all-comers, just to go down by your guns, Andrews? Let me tell you straight out—Stuart Campbell has no match at his kind of fighting."

"Maybe not," piped up weasel-face, who seemed to

112

be enjoying this exchange, "but he don't know Moses Andrews either, or the rest of us. Didn't none of us come down in the last rain either, Mister Holmes. We've all done our share of battlin'."

"I can imagine," said Russ dryly, skewering that crafty-eyed man with a cold stare. "But like I said, it's not worth getting killed over—just to prove you can fight—because when it's all over you still won't own any of Tocannon Valley."

One of the heretofore silent other men brought his thoughtful gaze back from a long survey of the afternoon-hazed vastness of Tocannon Valley and said to Russ, "It's a big place, Mister Holmes. Looks to me to be at least thirty miles long an' maybe fifteen miles wide. This Stuart Campbell don't claim all of it, does he?"

"No," answered Cliff Lefton. "Only the first ten square miles of it. All the upper end of the valley to the foot of this Pass. But that also happens to be the best-watered land with the deepest soil and finest grass, an' you fellers said it was Tocannon land you had claims on."

This same quiet-speaking lanky man spat aside, gazed at Cliff and said, "Mister; suppose we just ride on down an' ask to see that deed?"

Cliff looked helplessly around at Russ. The deed was many miles away by now. Russ started to explain that but weasel-face snorted his derision, saying, "Let's go on, Moses; I got a feelin' these two been sent up here to try an' hoodwink us. I don't believe there's any deed a-tall."

Russ felt his anger rising. This was the second time that same man had skirted perilously close to openly calling him a liar. He said to weasel-face, "Mind telling

113

me your name, mister?"

"Don't mind at all," snapped weasel-face. "It's Carl Wendt. An' now that you know what . . .?"

"Now that I know," cut in Russ coldly. "I'll remember it, Carl, because bein' called a liar doesn't set too well with me."

Moses Andrews' hard little smile vanished. He fixed Russ with a tough look and said, "You aren't figurin' on startin' this here fight right here an' now are you, Mister Holmes, because if you are then I'd say you got more guts than brains? The odds against you are sort of big— five to two."

"You like bein' called a liar, Mister Andrews?" challenged Russ.

Andrews didn't answer right away. His square, massive jaw jutted and his black eyes burnt brightly over at Russ. "Ain't no man called me one a long time," he said softly, his tone full of menace. Then he did what to Russ was an unexpected thing. He turned his head slightly and growled over at Carl Wendt: "Quit tryin' to push this into a fight."

Wendt wilted in his saddle. Suddenly, the big, tough man whom he was relying upon to support him had withdrawn that support, leaving Carl Wendt exposed for what he really was, not a very brave man.

Russ stared at Andrews, making some mental corrections in his initial appraisal of this rough, hard man. There seemed now to be another side to Andrews other than the willingly belligerent side. This raised Russs's hopes slightly and he said, "We can show you some well-watered campsites down in the valley that aren't on Campbell's land. Let us do that so there'll be no battle until tomorrow."

"Why tomorrow?" asked Andrews.

"Because Stuart Campbell's son'll be back from the county seat where he went to record Tocannon's deed by then, an' you'll get your proof there's no unclaimed land in the valley."

"How about the rest of the valley?" asked that lanky, thoughtful-looking man.

"All deeded land," said Cliff. "Every foot of it."

Andrews nodded at this statement; he seemed to Russ to already know this. Then he confirmed that suspicion by saying, "That much is true anyway. I looked at all the land-office maps. The only piece of Tocannon Valley that showed as free-claim land was this upper ten miles." Andrews paused, kept watching Russ from his shrewd, tough black eyes for a moment, then he shrugged, saying, "I ain't callin' no one a liar, Mister Holmes. All I'm sayin' is that we got five land-patents on five sections of land, and I don't think the government made any mistake. Now then, I figure to ride on down there and look up my homestead. You about half got me convinced there's been a mistake made somewhere, but on the other hand we didn't ride no thousand miles just to be turned back on one man's say-so."

There was a difference now in Moses Andrews' attitude. Russ recognized this at once and felt he'd have to compromise a little to meet it, so he reiterated his earlier proposal. He said, "All we're asking is that you stay off Tocannon Ranch range until tomorrow; that you camp somewhere east of the Pass so no fight starts."

"An' supposin' this here feller doesn't get back tomorrow?" asked Wendt. "Then what, Mister Holmes?"

"Then," said Russ, "I'll have done all I can do." He had known right from the beginning of this discussion

115

that if he'd asked for more time these rough men would have refused to give it to him. He also knew how thin the ice was underneath him even if Brigham *did* return by tomorrow because, aside from the conditioned truculence of these settlers, old Stuart would be riding up into the Pass any time now, and the moment Campbell saw any of these settlers—including Russ himself—he would start his private war.

He dared not say anything about this though; these five men were balancing upon the raw edge of violence as it was. If they had any inkling they might be attacked they very clearly wouldn't wait for that to happen. They were all heavily armed and willing to fight.

He said to Andrews: "Cliff and I'll ride on down with you." What he meant was that he and Lefton would take the settlers five miles east, or so far off Tocannon land that even if old Stuart located them, which was not probable providing they got down out of the Pass and eastward after dusk arrived, he might not feel impelled to attack them because they'd obviously be far away from his Tocannon range.

"Tell me something," said Moses Andrews wonderingly, "if you're a settler like you say, Mister Holmes, how is it that you're so all-fired keen on preventin' a meetin' between us and this old devil Stuart Campbell? Seems to me us settlers got more to gain by standin' shoulder to shoulder than by takin' opposite sides."

"That's simple," replied Russ, "Because I don't like the idea of men gettin' shot up needlessly. I saw all I want to see of that kind of killing during the war."

Andrews' gaze warmed up a little. "Well, well," he said, more to the men with him than to Russ or Cliff. "So you was in the war. As a matter of fact, Mister

116

Holmes, I was a sergeant in Cap'n Paine's First Minnesota Sharpshooters, and these other lads was also soldiers."

Russ breathed a quiet little sigh of relief. He'd inadvertently touched upon Moses Andrews' nostalgic soft spot. "Maybe we saw some of the same action," he suggested. "We can talk about this on the ride down, an' since it's getting near to sundown maybe we ought to start right now."

Without another dissenting word Andrews lifted his reins, nodded, and prodded his horse along. Russ and Cliff wheeled, fell in one either side of him and started the long descent.

# CHAPTER FIFTEEN

THEY TALKED ABOUT THE WAR, ALL OF THEM BUT Carl Wendt who seemed sullen over this comradeship which had sprung up in place of the earlier suspicion and skepticism. It seemed to Russ as though Wendt didn't want anything solved amicably, which was unusual, until he made a pointed, long study of the weasel-faced thin rider, then it became obvious that Wendt was one of those natural trouble-makers, one of those men who delighted in stirring up trouble for no better reason than because he liked to goad other men into actions which he, himself, quite lacked the courage to participate in.

The other settlers were different. They were hard men, the kind of men who had borne all the agony and anguish of four years of bitter campaigning stoically so that they might one day march through the streets of Richmond, in the Confederate State of Virginia, which they had done.

They were men whose characters had been forged and tempered in the crucible of a bloody war. They were not the type of men, Russ knew, who would run from some legendary old warrior like Stuart Campbell, for in their time they had vanquished other legendary fighters and they no longer frightened easily.

He said to Cliff, when they were half-way down the Pass, "Lope on ahead, Cliff, and do a little scouting." He accompanied this order with a long stare which Cliff understood as he nodded, slackened his reins and hooked his horse.

On Russ's left side Moses Andrews looked after Lefton gravely then said, "Why the precaution, Mister Holmes; you expectin' trouble down here?"

Russ shrugged. "Trouble could be a big drive of cattle outward bound through the Pass, or it could be a driven band of horses, Mister Andrews." He let it lie like that and although Moses Andrews looked around at him, Andrews also seemed content to leave it like that.

They rode along recalling incidents from the war, all of them but Carl Wendt turning easy and talkative as the shadows lengthened down in the Pass, as the overhead sky turned vermilion in the last red light of fading day.

Moses Andrews had been in most of the Peninsular battles. He had been wounded three times. He regaled them with tales which were sometimes too sad for tears, and which at other times were hilariously amusing.

As Russ rode along beside this big, bearded man, he completed his revision of opinion about Moses Andrews. There remained a solid conviction that Andrews would fight. The cause wouldn't even have to be very good; all Moses Andrews needed to go into action would be a slurred insult, a coarse word directed

118

at him, or a hint of someone trying to stand between him and what he wanted.

But where Russ had initially thought Moses Andrews might be a bully, he thought now that this wasn't so. What had appeared as bullying tactics up in the Pass seemed now to be simply the bearded's man's complete inability to put up with any interference in his personal plans. He was tough, uncompromising, and hard as iron. But he seemed to Russ to also be a fair man, so, as they neared the bottom of the Pass, Russ said, "Probably most of what you've been told about Stuart Campbell is true enough, Mister Andrews, but there's the other side too. He pioneered this country and it wasn't easy. He buried his wife here and raised his kids. He carved out a cow empire, pushed back the frontier, and he was both the law and the armed force in his part of Utah when you and I were in knee-breeches."

"I know the kind," said Andrews. "I knew Jim Bridger and Frenchy Sublette when I was a lad. I didn't come here seekin' no battle with Stuart Campbell, don't get me wrong on that score, Mister Holmes. But I sure come here prepared to fight if I had to."

Russ looked down where his crossed hands lay atop his saddlehorn. "So did I," he murmured. "You see, I stopped over in the settlements too. I heard the same stories about the lord of Tocannon Valley you fellers also heard."

"He showed you that there deed, Mister Holmes?"

Russ shook his head. "Never saw it although I could've if I'd wanted to."

"Then how come you're so sure there *is* a deed?"

"I'm the one who told Stuart's son to ride like the devil was behind him to the county seat and get it recorded."

Andrews and the other settler-men gazed in amazement at Russ. "What the hell kind of sense does that make?" challenged Carl Wendt. "I told you what the law says. First man to lay claim an' file owns the land."

Russ looked briefly at the weasel-faced man then looked around at the others, finally holding his gaze upon the darkly hairy face of Moses Andrews. "The notion of claimin' another man's property just because some damned technicality of the law makes it legal to do so doesn't much appeal to me," he said. "And there's another reason to. In fact there are several other reasons. But let's just say I admire what old Stuart's dedicated his lifetime to creating. I only wish I'd had his foresight and his courage."

"You know him well?" Andrews asked.

"Not well," answered Russ, his face turning sardonic. "In fact the first time we ever met I called him. The second time he tried to get me killed."

"But you're stickin' up for him? Holmes, I just plain don't understand you," said Andrews with a rough wag of his head.

Russ rode along for a hundred yards saying nothing, and if he afterwards meant to speak he didn't get the chance because Cliff came jogging on up towards them and in the soft-lighted early evening Russ could make out the anxious and disturbed expression upon Lefton's face. Without allowing Cliff time to say what was bothering him, Russ threw him a dark scowl and at the same time flagged off eastward with his upraised right arm.

"Leave the road here," he said to Andrews, "cut on down into the foothills through that open country over there. It'll save a lot of time an' it'll soon be dark."

Andrews and the others looked off in the indicated

120

direction where there was no visible trail but where the lower-down country lay open and gently rolling. Without another word Russ eased off in that direction leading the way. He didn't turn to gaze over at Cliff again until they'd passed along nearly a quarter of a mile, and by then the settlers including burly Moses Andrews were busy herding their pack animals.

Russ drew off a little way and came up beside Cliff. He again didn't give Cliff a chance to speak first. "Let me guess," he dryly said, "old Stuart's coming."

"Coming hell," growled Cliff. "He's already past the first bend in the roadway back there by this time." Cliff scowled. "Why'd you cut me off like that?"

"To keep you from saying anything that'd get our friends all fired up to fight again."

"Well hell," grumbled Cliff. "Stuart'll see the tracks where we left the cussed trail."

Russ rode a little distance twisted in his saddle looking back. "Maybe not," he eventually said. "If he's still in that same all-fired hurry to get up the Pass he might ride right on past." He squared back around and looked ahead where the others were getting their pack animals lined out. "Just give us one more hour and it'll be too dark for him to track us anyway."

"Humph," grunted Cliff, still nettled at being turned aside like that. "Stuart Campbell can *smell* tracks, he don't have to see 'em."

"You better hope you're wrong, Cliff. Was he alone or did he have someone with him?"

"He was alone," replied Cliff, then, watching the fresh course Andrews' men were taking he said, "Say; have you any idea where them fellers are heading?"

"No idea at all," stated Russ amiably. "I've never been east of the Pass."

"Then," said Cliff dourly, "you'd better let me take the lead, because if they keep on the way they're goin' now they're goin' to wind up in a swamp."

Russ told Cliff to lope on ahead but not to mention having sighted old Stuart, and he afterwards jogged back on up to ride stirrup with Moses Andrews. The bearded ex-infantryman watched Cliff take the lead, made a little frown and said, "What's botherin' him; he acts like he's in a hurry to get us out of these foothills."

"He is," stated Russ blandly. "There's a swamp up ahead. He doesn't want you blundering into it in the dark."

Andrews' face cleared and he relaxed in the saddle. For a full mile he rode along beside Russ watching Cliff and alternately looking back where his companions were guiding the pack-animals, and for that full distance on down to the valley floor he was silent.

The red evening was darkening now, turning sooty over against the bulwark hills where tiers of stiff-topped pines and firs stood in solid ranks. Andrews viewed those stands of timber and made a practical observation.

"Plenty of everything here a man'd need to build himself quite a house and barn, Mister Holmes."

And Russ softly agreed, thinking of his own recent labors, thinking too how all he'd created lay now in blackened ruins. Then he repeated what he'd heard Brigham Campbell tell that other band of squatters.

"South of Tocannon Valley there is a lot of good free land that hasn't been taken up yet. Trees and water down there too."

This seemed to fill some void in Moses Andrews' thoughts because the bearded man turned towards Russ looking interested, looking speculative. "You don't say," he murmured. "Plenty of water too?"

122

Russ nodded. "I reckon it won't be free much longer though. Just yesterday four men rode through bound down in that direction. They had pack outfits along too."

"Four," mused Andrews. "Four men couldn't make much of a dent in a big slice of open land."

Russ, watching Cliff, saw the Tocannon cowboy veer over towards the eastward hills. He was confident Cliff would take them to a good camp-site. He was also grateful Cliff was along because Russ didn't know this country over here east of Winchester Pass at all.

"Tell me," said Moses Andrews. "How'd you come to want to settle here, Mister Holmes?"

Russ explained about coming into the valley as a drover years before, and how he'd always remembered the Tocannon country as an ideal place to settle.

"And now . . .?" asked Andrews.

Russ shrugged. "Maybe I'll go on down south with you fellers," he said. "I don't know yet; haven't thought that far ahead."

Andrews thought this over and gravely inclined his head. "We'd be right proud to have you join us," he said, and turned as one of the others trotted up to say something about one of the horses getting a little lame. Andrews at once turned out to ride back up along the file of animals with this man to inspect the limping horse, and Russ had a chance to be free for a little while. He loped on ahead where Cliff was. It was by this time turning quite dark. Not because day was done so much as because as they neared the forested far hillsides on across the valley shadows lay deeper and darker, made that way by the gloomy forests.

"How much further?" he asked.

Cliff shrugged. "Water's about a mile ahead. That

ought to do it. We'll be about four miles east of the trace. What do you think?"

"Good enough," agreed Russ. "And I'm going back as soon as they make camp. You stay with them."

"You goin' to try an' out-Indian old Stuart?"

"I'm at least going to try an' keep him from coming over in this direction."

Cliff shook his head. "I been thinking," he said. "You'll have to be able to see in the dark, Russ. Sooner or later these here fellers'll light up a cookin' fire. He'll spot that sure as the devil. But even if they didn't make no fire on a still night like this old Stuart'll hear their horses."

Russ had also thought of these contingencies. That was precisely why he meant to go back and try hard to prevent Stuart from coming along eastward from Winchester Pass. He said, "You keep 'em in camp if they act like they want to walk out a ways in the dark. If I run into anything I can't handle . . ." Russ shrugged and gazed knowingly over at Cliff. "We've done more than I figured we'd be lucky enough to accomplish, Cliff. All we can do now is try and find Stuart before he finds them, and hamstring him some way."

"Won't be easy, Russ. Like I been sayin', that old man's more Injun than white when he's roiled up. And believe me, today's been a bad day for him. The only way I figure you'll be able to do anything with him, is if you can find him 'thout him hearin' or seeing you. And that, my friend, I just don't believe you can do."

Moses Andrews came trotting up. He looked at Cliff and looked on ahead. "How much further to water?" he asked.

Cliff pointed straight on ahead through the gathering gloom. "You could hit water with a stone from where we are right now, Mister Andrews. I reckon you can tell them other fellers they can stop any time now."

They came to a little creek which tumbled down out of the onward forest and halted. Russ, viewing that brawling rush of white-water, was reminded of the stream over near where he'd built his log-house—over where he'd buried Joe Mesa.

As the settlers got stiffly down and spoke back and forth to one another over the good fortune they'd had in finding a place with both good water and good grass, Russ dismounted and stood beside his horse. Once, when mighty Moses Andrews started past, he called him over and said, "I'm goin' back a ways, but I'll return in an hour or so."

Andrews stood stock-still considering Russ. Finally he said, "You've been expectin' something since we left the trail. Want me to ride back with you?"

Russ shook his head. "I can handle this better alone. And it may not be anything anyway. But if you boys'll save me a little supper I'll be grateful. Seems to me I've postponed about three, four meals up to now."

Andrews nodded approval. "There'll be food when you get back." He pushed forth a ham of a hand. "Reckon I had you pegged wrong, Holmes. I apologize ."

Russ shook, smiled, turned and re-mounted. As he walked his horse back up the rearward trail the others turned to setting up camp.

# CHAPTER SIXTEEN

THE LAND LAY QUIET IN ITS DUSKY SHROUD AND FOR A mile Russ was fortunate; his shod-horse did not strike stone. He thought it unlikely old Stuart would have returned from his search up towards Winchester Pass's crest yet, but on the other hand he wanted to find the old cowman before Stuart sighted a cooking fire far down and easterly. If he didn't, he considered it unlikely that he'd be able to intercept Campbell before Stuart rode on over and hit the settler-camp.

He had two advantages and one serious disadvantage. It was too dark now for the older man to see tracks or see Russ, and Stuart would not suspect he was being hunted. He would consider himself the hunter.

The disadvantage was that old Stuart knew this land and Russ did not know it. It was one thing to seek a man in flat country, it was something altogether different to hunt a man in mountainous country.

But there were the obvious ways and Russ relied upon them. He halted often to test the night, to listen closely and also keep a sharp watch for movement.

When he came within sight of the road he hid his horse among some trees and went ahead on foot. He found a good vantage point and lay flat up there waiting for movement. This place was slightly more than half-way up the Pass. If old Stuart didn't cut off eastward through the hills, and there was as yet no reason for him to do this, then the chances were powerfully in favor of his turning about and heading back down the Pass.

Russ knew that while old Stuart had returned to the Pass because he thought Russ was still somewhere in

126

the vicinity, it would be only a matter of time before those settlers down there made their supper fire and Stuart would spot that. Whether he thought the fire might belong to Russ or not wasn't too important because he'd scout that fire, see the heavily-armed strangers, and easily deduce whom they were and what their intention was in coming into the valley. After that he'd follow the course of action he'd used against other squatters, with one exception: This time old Stuart wouldn't have his Tocannon men to back his play.

What looked to Russ like a huge coyote went trotting past, soft starshine turning his silvery fur almost white. The beast caught a scent, skidded to a halt and stood a long moment sniffing. He had his tongue out and lolling; it was a warm night. Then the animal took several tentative steps in Russ's direction, but he was thirty feet lower down and seemed a little puzzled by the obvious man-scent he was picking up because it appeared to come from the overhead air.

Then Russ got a good look at this animal and saw that it wasn't a large coyote at all, it was a bitch-wolf and she was swollen with pup, near her whelping time. He picked up a rock and tossed it downhill. At the first sound of that stone striking down the she-wolf spun and fled with an agility and speed her ungainly size made it initially appear she would be incapable of. In a twinkling she was gone, the night settled back into its pattern of age-old silence and stillness, skimmer-owls swooped along without a sound watching for night-feeding rodents, the moon firmed up in its first quarter giving even less light than the stars, and Russ heard an iron horseshoe strike ancient stone on up the pass.

He pinpointed the direction of that horse. It seemed to be coming diagonally on across the trail bearing eastward. There could be just one reason for this so he turned up onto his side, looked backwards and downwards, and saw the same little yellow flicker of a fire far away which had evidently attracted the invisible horseman. The settlers were making their long-delayed supper. Glowing softly in a pale yellow way against that close-packed dense darkness of the backgrounding forest, that small fire put a high, soft light upwards and outwards into the night.

Russ lay still a moment longer thinking. Old Stuart would make for that fire, certainly. The trick now would be for Russ to get ahead of him and stay ahead until he had a good sighting, then jump Campbell before he could in turn attack the settlers.

He got down off his vantage point without a sound and glided back to the place where his patient horse was waiting. He could no longer hear Stuart, which didn't entirely surprise him. After half a century of riding these hills the old devil would know every inch of this countryside; where there would be outcroppings of rock Stuart would avoid them, where he could be skylined by sentinels, he would keep clear. What Cliff Lefton had gloomily prophesied came back to bother Russ now. Cliff hadn't thought Russ could out-Indian old Campbell.

He got astride and studied the ghostly northward lifts and rises. There was one long trace where a man riding eastward would never have the paler sky behind him. He took his long chance and rode across that route. He was sitting motionless among some scrub-oaks when he heard the soft chukkering sound a horse makes when he clears his nostrils. It was lower down and almost parallel with him. He reined out in that direction, hadn't gone a hundred yards when his own animal blundered over a shale-rock outcropping and sent forth its own telegraphing sounds of steel over stone.

At once all sound and movement down below faded out. Russ swung out of the saddle quickly, unwilling to risk being skylined by old Stuart and shot for his carelessness. He left his animal tied to a manzanita bush and with his carbine in both hands glided on over that shale-rock field, struck grassy soil again and kept on advancing towards the place where he'd last heard old Stuart.

It was a prickly business being on the offensive in this unfamiliar, gloomy place, with all his meager advantages gone now. He considered calling out, trying to talk his way up close enough to rush Campbell. He didn't do this because instinct warned him against doing anything that would reveal his whereabouts. Old Stuart Campbell would not, under these circumstances, be a merciful man. This was his way of waging war. It was also the old-time Indian way. If an enemy was foolhardy enough to reveal himself, he would be killed, and neither the old-time redmen nor Stuart Campbell figured this to be a dishonorable method of fighting a foe.

He dropped low twice as he advanced, trying to sight a silhouette against the paler sky. Both times he was disappointed. Wherever that old devil was waiting, he was lying low and completely still. He was no longer on horseback either. Russ didn't know this to be true, but he felt that it was. Their silent battle was now being waged strictly man to man.

He picked up a stone and hurled it. He heard the stone strike but that was all he heard. He tried another ruse—deliberately dragging his rifle-barrel over rock to give the impression this had been thoughtlessly done, then he dropped down and swiftly rolled away.

But no shot came.

He lay in the acrid grass sweating. Somewhere close by a cold pair of deadly eyes were waiting and watching. The stars indifferently cast earthward their pewter light. That scimitar-like curved little moon floated overhead in its purple sea, and once a falling star scratched Infinity with a little glowing tailrace of hot light, then it winked out and nothing was changed by its violent passing.

Up near the limits of Winchester Pass a coyote mournfully tongued at the high vault of heaven making the world seem ancient beyond reckoning, unchanged since his first ancestor trotted the earth, and at any other time Russ would have listened to that haunting cry with his thoughts turning back through time, but now he only wondered what old Stuart's private reaction was to that sound, and he inched closer towards the spot where he'd heard that horse clear its nostrils. It seemed to Russ that he and the older man out here with him were the only mortals under a dark heaven.

But this was a teeming world. Nature held sway in these secret places. Her creatures were everywhere, some crawled, some slithered and some winged low through the silent night, and it was nature who gave Russ his first warning when a little boomer-hawk swept past, low and swift, holding a true course onward towards the rearward roadway while he night-hunted. Russ saw this little bird with its long, arched wings gliding westward from the corner of his eye. He saw the little boomer suddenly veer frantically and beat the air in a desperate attempt to gain altitude. Directly below the hawk was a stand of scrubby pines in a sunken place.

Russ halted, pushed his carbine ahead, and put his

entire attention upon those little scrubby trees. That boomer-hawk had seen something of which he was mortally fearful. It had to be a man. No other animal on legs inspired such dread in birds as well as all other animals.

For a while Russ lay still watching those trees trying hard to separate one shadow from another. He knew where old Stuart was lying low now, playing his waiting game. He considered his own situation. Evidently Stuart did not know exactly where Russ was, and that was an advantage, but the moment Russ made an aggressive move towards that clump of scrub-pines, old Stuart would fire. It was, in Russ's view, a standoff. He couldn't move and old Stuart wouldn't move. He let a full five minutes pass then returned to his original notion of trying to talk his way up. He could come up with no other solution.

"Campbell," he said, speaking swiftly so as to hold the older man's attention long enough to say what he wished to get across before he was fired upon. "Listen to me for just one minute. I know where you are in those trees. Brigham and Petl found that old Ute treaty giving you your ten square miles of Tocannon Valley. Brigham's gone to the county seat to have that deed recorded. It's the only legal way you can gain title to your land. Those men east of us are ex-soldiers who have land-claims. Yesterday Brigham and I met another band of them. We talked that bunch out of even trying to claim any Tocannon land, but this bunch isn't going to give up that easily. They've come all the way from Colorado and in the settlements they've heard stories of how you've held your range so far. They're ready to fight you. Cliff Lefton and I deliberately guided them off your range and over against the easterly hills to

131

prevent fighting. We're trying to hold them off until Brigham gets back with a copy of the recorded deed. If we can do that there won't be any need for fighting. Give us a chance to make this work, Campbell."

For a long while there was no word from old Stuart. Russ began to have a deep-down fear that old Stuart wasn't over there after all. Then that gruff, cold and unmistakable voice came back uttering just one word.

"Why?"

Russ didn't know whether Stuart meant why was Russ doing this or why should old Stuart hold off. He took a chance Campbell meant the former and said, "For your daughter's sake as well as for your own sake, Campbell."

"No, Holmes, it's more than that. You've turned them all against me. Even Petl. I tried to tell her how wrong you were down at your homestead and she wouldn't listen. If you sent Brigham to the county seat it had to be for some other reason. Why should you help me? I burnt you out."

"I know that," said Russ, beginning to hope. "But I'd already told Brigham I'd recognize that old Ute deed, so the house and the homestead revert to you."

"You're lying, Holmes. No man is that charitable towards an enemy."

"Think what you like," responded Russ. "Just don't try anything against those settlers down there until tomorrow. Give Brigham a chance to get back first."

"What have you done with that feller I brought back with me?"

"He's under guard in the smoke-house down at Tocannon Ranch."

"I paid him two hundred and fifty dollars advance to kill you, Holmes. Now tell me you didn't know about

132

that, if you captured him!"

"I found out about it. He volunteered to return the money if I'd let him ride back where he came from. Listen, Campbell; forget all that. It's tomorrow that counts. When Brigham gets back he can explain to you what all of us have done to save you from ruining yourself."

"You've turned them all against me, Holmes, an' I burnt you out for that. You hate my guts and you're using Petl an' the others to strike back. I think I know what you're trying to do; those men down there aren't here by accident. They're friends of yours. And I don't believe that about Brigham riding to the county seat either. What have you done with him, Holmes, buried him like you did Joe Mesa?"

Russ raised up to hotly deny all this just as Stuart fired. He'd been making his careful calculations all the while Russ had been talking and that bullet struck solidly into some gravelly soil ten feet ahead of Russ showering him with stinging splinters of granite and a cascading little gust of musty earth. He dropped flat, rolled downhill and dug at his eyes to clear them.

The echo of that gunshot rolled flatly up and over the surrounding hilltops sounding unusually loud because of the otherwise night-hush.

Old Stuart got off another shot too, but he no longer knew where Russ was so this one sang harmlessly through the night. He worked his carbine's mechanism and Russ heard stones rattle as old Stuart changed positions.

He had his eyes cleared by then. They copiously watered but gradually his good vision returned, and he was mad clear through, not entirely because he'd been fired upon but because of the stubborn suspicion he'd encountered. He poked his Winchester out, snugged it back against his shoulder and fired off three rounds as rapidly as he could lever and squeeze off each shot, then he dropped still further down the slope and stayed flat.

Old Stuart drove two more bullets straight into the night. Russ heard them rip into the ground where he'd been when he'd fired back at the older man. He gave old Stuart his due; not many men were this accurate in the dark.

The silence descended again, the last angry echo died out, Russ lay flat breathing hard and straining to detect movement. He heard none but as the minutes passed he became convinced old Stuart was getting away. He tried a shot. When no answering blast came back he knew the older man was indeed getting clear. He began to hastily work his way back to where he'd left his horse. When he found the animal he jumped astride and headed out for the settler camp. Somewhere in the night old Stuart was making for that same site.

# CHAPTER SEVENTEEN

RUSS GOT HALF-WAY BACK TOWARDS THE SETTLER-camp but he no longer had any light to travel by, for evidently at the first exchange of gunfire those seasoned fighting men down there had killed their cooking-fire.

Still, he knew the direction and the way back and he kept to them until, confident he would be ahead of old Stuart, he dropped a quarter mile down into the rolling, bald foothills and rode into a wide place between two hills where he dismounted and took his carbine with him as he scrambled atop a bare knoll.

He was now between the settlers and Stuart

134

Campbell. There was no other way for Campbell to approach that camp without going miles out of his way, up and around and down through the eastward trees, and even then he'd still have a mile or more of open valley land to cross. He would know all this, Russ speculated, and he wouldn't do that; he'd come straight down into these bald hills where Russ was waiting.

The settler-camp was now less than a half-mile south-eastward. There was a wispy scent of cooked food and charred wood in the air. It brought up all Russ's suppressed hunger in a rush. He'd been a long while without food and in fact, except for the acid sensation behind his belt, he'd scarcely been aware of his hunger until now.

A mounted man appeared northward where the last sage and buckbrush grew. Russ looked and wondered at this total recklessness. Old Stuart had evidently thrown caution to the wind now, probably, Russ thought, because he believed their earlier encounter had alerted all his enemies anyway.

Russ thought this was also so; he had no way of knowing how Moses Andrews and the others would react to those previous sounds of battle because he didn't know any of those men well enough to predict their courses of action. But one thing he was confident of was the simple and elemental fact that, being seasoned warriors, they wouldn't be sitting down there waiting to be attacked.

It stuck in his mind what he'd promised Petl. That he wouldn't kill her father. But it also crossed his mind now that Andrews and his companions would have no such compunction, and this made it more difficult than ever for Russ. He had to some way prevent old Stuart from attacking the settlers while at the same time trying

135

to keep from being killed by old Stuart himself, and also, he had to keep Andrews and the others from getting to old Stuart first.

It would have been much simpler, he grimly told himself, just to have been an out and out enemy of Stuart Campbell.

He lay there watching that stalwart old man atop his horse over on that brush-fringed hill thinking that Stuart was acting more Indian than ever. It was the old-time Ute custom to ride up against the skyline and sit grimly where an enemy could see him and be cowed by his deadly intent. The old devil was far beyond carbine range though, so at least for now he was safe. Then he abruptly turned his horse, dropped straight down into a concealing canyon and seemed to Russ to be heading straight down towards the settler-camp.

It required several minutes for Russ to make his survey of the landforms here so that he could determine which route was available to Stuart, but after he had that figured out he left his hillock, trotted back to his horse, sprang up and reined off easterly to intercept him again. He hadn't covered more than a quarter mile when he saw a man on foot glide forth from around a bald hill. He knew instinctively this would be one of the settlers but he didn't know which one. He hissed, making that intent onward silhouette whip upright and whirl towards him. The second starlight touched down across that thin, long face, Russ recognized Carl Wendt. He rode on up and swung down. Wendt was darkly and suspiciously scowling at him.

"Where are the others?" Russ asked.

Wendt jerked his head. "Back by the camp but fanned out against the nearest foothills. We thought he might've plugged you."

Russ's brows drew inward. "Who might've plugged

136

me, Wendt?"

The weasel-faced man's expression turned sly and knowing. "Lefton told us what you fellers been tryin' to keep from happening. It's old Stuart Campbell. I seen him a minute ago sittin' up there on one of them northward hills as bold as brass. If he does that again I'll drive six ounces of lead right through his damned guts."

"How come you're this far out if the others are making a line back by the camp?"

"I was takin' first turn at sentry-go when we heard the firin' over westward near the Pass. I been scoutin' since then, that's how come I'm so far north o' camp." Wendt grounded his carbine and leaned upon it studying Russ's face in the watery light. "Cliff told us about you'n the old man's daughter too. Maybe that gives you reason for not wantin' him knocked off, but it doesn't influence me one damned bit, Holmes."

"Let me handle him, Wendt. That's why I left camp in the first place. I think I can get him before he does you fellers any harm."

"Not by a damned sight, Holmes. You been takin' the others in ever since we first met, but not me, by gawd." Wendt lifted his carbine, held it across his upper body in both hands and turned his head left and right rummaging the silent night.

For a moment Russ stared at the settler. He balanced a sudden notion in his mind and when Carl Wendt was peering intently northward Russ drew his .45, chopped it overhand in a savage little arc and brought it hard down across Wendt's skull. Without a sound the settler fell all in a heap.

Russ emptied the man's carbine, pocketed the shells. He stuck Wendt's six-gun into his own waistband and he tossed Wendt's shell-belt away in the night. He stood a moment broodingly gazing at the slack bundle of humanity at his feet, then he shrugged and walked back to his horse.

If Andrews and the others were holding a line nearer camp it meant they were prudently staying close to their packs and their pack-animals while they awaited old Stuart's coming, and now, with Carl Wendt out of the way, Russ was still the only person between Stuart and the settlers, with all the initiative. It was anything but an enviable position but in order to accomplish what he was at least dedicated to trying, it was his only way.

He rode back up the swale past Wendt's loose form and scarcely cast a look downward. If he should have felt remorse he didn't.

There were odd shadows up in here where hilltops cut off the overhead light turning the soft night into a stygian place of total darkness here and there. When he thought he was about even with old Stuart's down-country course he left his horse and went ahead on foot as he'd done before.

It was a good idea. He hadn't progressed a hundred yards when he saw a lank shadow fade out in formless night at his approach. He knelt, took long aim and fired about where a man's legs would be. Instantly a six-gun roared and flame lanced outwards at him in a mushrooming fashion.

Stuart's shot was too far to the right but evidently Russ's bullet was close because there came next the grinding-down sound of booted feet swiftly moving. He tracked that sound and fired again, still holding low. This time he got back no return-fire, only a hooting high call of strong derision. Old Stuart was playing with him.

He got up into a low crouch and darted back and forth as he steadily ran ahead. Where the side-hill loomed up showing pale in the moonlight because of its matting of cured, dry grass, he angled along it seeking to get above Stuart. This was a grave mistake because the old cowman, anticipating some such tactic, was waiting down there. The moment Russ left the lower-down darkness and was backgrounded by that light-colored grass, old Stuart fired at him.

Russ dropped straight down and rolled back downhill with Stuart trying to pot-shoot him as he rolled. Dirt burst upwards around him and when he finally got back into the darkness and tried to stand, one leg crumpled under him.

He sat down wondering why there was no pain. What he discovered was that a bullet had expertly sheared off one boot-heel leaving him with one long leg and one short leg.

He rolled up onto his stomach and plumbed the night, picked up sounds parallel to him but down below as though Stuart was seeking to fight past Russ to get at the settlers, and he fired at those sounds.

As before, the older man evidently had been waiting just such an action for the second Russ's carbine flamed, he shot straight back with his .45. This time the bullet drew blood; it struck Russ's carbine barrel wrenching the gun violently sideways. It followed along the groove between magazine and barrel, smashed into the wooden stock and sent a sliver deep into Russ's hand.

He grunted with shock, with pain, dropped the ruined Winchester and tugged out the walnut splinter. Blood gushed into his left hand puddling swiftly in the palm. He clenched that fist to minimise the bleeding, drew his six-gun and turned with cold wrath towards the area that gunshot had come from.

But old Stuart was also utilizing the formless night

next to that shielding hill. Russ knew he was down there but could see nothing of him, not even reflected light off a pistol barrel.

His hand and wrist ached. They were dark with sticky blood and he was at last wholly angry towards Petl's father. He jumped up and ran down the hill. Stuart fired twice at him, missed both times, and was himself fired upon by Russ, driving the fierce old cowman further away from his hillside.

"You want a fight, damn you," cried Russ. "Now stand up and fight!"

He ran straight for the place he'd last spotted those muzzleblasts, firing as he went. Old Stuart could not face this deadly volley, no flesh and blood could have stood up to it and survived. Stuart turned and ran out where soft starshine caught him, making his first mistake of the night.

Russ saw Campbell finally and halted to throw up his .45, track that twisting, turning figure, and squeeze off a shot. Stuart sprang high into the air, half-turned and came down facing fully around. He snapped back an answering shot. Russ involuntarily flinched from the lethal whisper as that bullet came within inches of his face, then he fired again, jumped back out of the way and dropped to one knee. He had to re-load.

As he worked he kept alternately watching Stuart and concentrating upon the work at hand. The older man stood out there bracing forward. He fired once more but after that he seemed to have lost contact with Russ, seemed to be swinging his head back and forth seeking to re-locate his enemy. But what struck Russ as totally foolish and unlike a man of his kind, old Stuart made no attempt to run back into the cloying darkness.

He finished re-loading, cocked his six-gun and aimed

it. Something was tugging at the back of his mind, but because he was thoroughly angry now he only half-heeded this little nagging sensation. He fired once more, his target dead ahead and still unmoving. He saw Stuart wince, saw him stagger. But Campbell threw back another shot driving Russ flat down again. Now, however, Russ heeded that small and persistent voice. He'd hit the cowman with that former shot, had some way rendered old Stuart incapable of further flight. He knew he'd also scored with that second shot; a man might wince from a near-hit but he seldom staggered from one. The reason that stubborn old devil out there had staggered was because he'd also been struck by Russ's second and last shot.

Into the tense silence now came a bull-bass rumbling voice from off on Russ's right. He recognized the voice almost as soon as it called out.

"Hold it. You two battlers up there—hold it!"

This was bearded, tough and knowledgeable Moses Andrews. Russ hadn't, until Andrews called out, considered that his running scrape with old Stuart had put them both close enough down-country towards the open valley-floor country to be under the observation of the settlers.

"Holmes?" sang out Andrews in his rough voice. "Holmes; you hurt?"

Russ was watching old Stuart out there as he answered. Campbell seemed bewildered, seemed unable to decide what he must do now. His gun-arm was hanging straight down and his fierce old face was gazing off in the direction of Andrews' voice.

"Hey, Holmes; can you hear me? Are you hurt?"

"No," answered Russ. "Not's so you'd notice it. Andrews? Don't fire on him. He's hit."

141

"I know that, dammit," came back Andrews' waspish answer. "Is he that there Stuart Campbell?"

"Yes," said Russ. "Now hold on, I'm goin' over to him."

"Don't be a fool, Holmes. Wait until he drops. He's on the verge of it now. Just sit back there where he can't see you and wait him out."

Russ was considering the good logic of this advice when old Stuart turned squarely towards the sound of Andrews' voice and called forth a sizzling epithet. "You damned filthy land-grabbers, step out where I can see you an' we'll settle this man to man. Come out into sight, you scum!"

Someone down there with Andrews took umbrage at those blistering epithets and growled a profane reply, but it was Moses Andrews whose voice came back clearest; it was neither angry nor particularly bleak.

"Get it all out of your system, old man," Andrews said evenly. "We got all the time in the world. Tonight an' tomorrow if need be, and tomorrow night too. We got water and grub—and a fat hill to duck behind, so cuss and rant all you want, Campbell, because you're goin' to run out of cuss words and blood at about the same time."

Russ, watching old Stuart, was reminded of a brave old lion brought to bay, hurt and stubbornly refusing to believe he was beaten, but vanquished nonetheless. His rancour slowly atrophied, turned sour in his mouth, so he holstered his six-gun and did as the others were also doing, waited for old Stuart to fall.

It was a long wait. Campbell went down to one knee. He went down on both knees, but he kept swinging his head for a target fully ten minutes before Russ saw him wilt, slump over and slide out face-down his full length in the dead grass.

# CHAPTER EIGHTEEN

RUSS WAS ALREADY BENDING OVER OLD STUART WHEN Andrews and three other settlers walked up with drawn guns. He rolled the fierce old cowman over so the others could see where those two bullets had struck him.

"Once in the left leg, once in the right leg," observed Moses Andrews, and tugged at his beard. "That was gallant of you, Mister Holmes, but it wasn't exactly good sense. This old man was out to kill you."

Cliff Lefton stepped around Andrews and also dropped to one knee. Cliff looked at old Stuart with a guilty expression. It required no vast knowledge of cowboys to understand Lefton's mixed feelings; he'd taken sides against his employer which was, among cowmen, one of the worst crimes a man could commit.

"We better get him back to camp," Cliff mumbled, but made no immediate move to lift old Stuart. "He's plumb unconscious."

Russ took away the old man's gun and until he tried to push it into his waistband where it struck against Carl Wendt's gun which was already there, he had completely forgotten the other gun.

He stood up, plucked forth Wendt's .45 and handed it across to Moses Andrews. "Belongs to Wendt," he said, looking at those solemn faces around him in the moonlight. "I knocked him over the head back by the first northward hill."

Andrews took the gun and looked from it to Russ. "Wendt," he said in a surprised-sounding voice. "You knocked *Wendt* over the head?"

"He was dead-set on killing Stuart Campbell. I had to knock him over the head."

One of the others abruptly turned and started walking back down towards that distant little hillock where Wendt still lay. Moses Andrews said no more on the subject but he didn't look at all pleased as he returned his gaze to the unconscious gaunt older man at their feet.

They picked old Stuart up and took him back to the darkened camp where someone re-built the fire and set on a pot of coffee. For a while there wasn't much said, then one of the settlers came walking slowly into camp supporting Carl Wendt, whose face had been bruised when he'd fallen after being struck down, and whose eyes full of pain and rancour. Wendt reached for the hip-holstered gun of Moses Andrews who was standing close by the moment he saw Russ bending over old Stuart working at stopping Campbell's bleeding. But Moses turned with a growl and clapped a ham-like paw over that gun preventing Wendt from taking it.

"Leave be," he said to Wendt. "It's all over now."

"Not for me it ain't," snarled Carl Wendt, shaking free from the arm of the man who'd helped him back into camp. "That Holmes feller struck me down when m'back was turned. I want some satisfaction for that, by gawd!"

Russ looked up, watched Wendt's bruised, wild-eyed face a moment, then said to Cliff Lefton who was there beside him, "Finish tyin' them off hard," and stood up facing the irate settler. He dug deep into a trouser pocket, brought forth a little roll of paper money, peeled off five ten dollar bills and pushed them over at Wendt. Fifty dollars was a lot of money.

"To buy headache remedy with," Russ said quietly. "I'm sorry I had to do that but you said you wanted to kill him and I had my reasons for keepin' him alive.

144

Take the money."

Wendt took it, counted it with a dark scowl and his covetous little sly eyes began at once to lose most of their indignation. He pushed the bills into a trouser pocket.

Moses Andrews, watching this exchange, abruptly turned his back on Wendt. It was abundantly clear to everyone the moment Wendt accepted Russ's money Andrews considered the matter closed. So did the others, who suited their looks and actions to Andrews'.

Cliff was finished with the bandaging, was starting to stand up, when one of the men said, "Coffee's ready," and stepped across where the fire was merrily crackling. Russ and Cliff also turned. Then Russ suddenly halted to cock his head. Andrews saw this and also paused to listen. He said, "Rider comin'." He rapped that out in a tough way that alerted everyone. They all moved well clear of that backgrounding little fire and dropped their hands hipward.

"If it's an enemy," someone growled, "he's kind of bold, ridin' right on in like this all alone."

"It won't be an enemy," said Russ, beginning to believe he knew who this would be, and he was right. Petl came slow-pacing her horse out of the darkness. As soon as firelight touched her face the settler-men stood transfixed. They'd had no idea so lovely a girl was anywhere around, and in fact until she appeared they hadn't had a solitary thought about girls.

She swung down, saw old Stuart bandaged and lying there, walked over without glancing at the stalwart men standing grimly around watching, and she dropped down beside her father. She listened to his breathing, considered the crude but adequate bandages, got up and walked back out to her horse, still ignoring all those

145

men. After rummaging in a saddlebag briefly she returned once more to old Stuart and this time she looked up.

"Help me," she murmured to Russ. "Hold his head up."

Russ dropped down to obey and Petl held up a bottle of whisky. They got three large swallows down Stuart and Russ eased him back down very gently, saying as he did this, "He'll make it, Petl. They're both in his legs. Shock more than anything else knocked him out."

"You put them there, Russ?" she asked, gazing somberly up at him.

"Yes. I couldn't prevent his being killed any other way."

She nodded as Moses Andrews, standing aside tugging at his beard, said, "Little lady, Mister Holmes done the gallant thing. Your paw tried his dangdest to kill him. I don't think another man would've risked his life twice to keep from killing someone as hell-bent on doin' him in as your father was. I know for a fact I wouldn't have. Now you'd better leave the old devil rest and have some black coffee with us."

Petl got up slowly. She was still holding that quart of whisky. Russ took her arm and steered her on over to the fire where a settler offered her a tin cup. Not until she reached forth to take it and saw the bottle in her hand did she seem to recollect having the liquor. She turned, looked into Moses Andrews' fiercely bearded countenance and handed him the whisky.

"I suppose it wouldn't hurt to pour a little into the coffee, would it?" she asked.

Andrews' strong white teeth shone in an appreciative grin. "Wouldn't hurt a thing," he agreed, and took the bottle.

They sat quiet for a long time. Even Carl Wendt seemed to have recovered from his headache. After a while they spoke softly back and forth, sometimes including Petl in their questions and comments, sometimes including Russ.

A little ahead of dawn Russ volunteered to head on over to Tocannon Ranch for a wagon and team to transport old Stuart on down to his burnt-out homestead with, where the doctor could re-bandage old Stuart's injuries.

Petl demurred saying Russ was worn out, that he'd already done more than she and her brother could ever hope to repay him for, and that she would go after the wagon. Moses Andrews gallantly offered to accompany her but she refused this offer too, with a little smile, and shortly afterwards rode off with the eastern sky beginning to burn with a pale glow high up along the sawtooth mountain rims.

Some of Andrews' men fell upon their blankets and exhaustedly slept. Russ walked over with Cliff Lefton and stood above old Stuart for a while thinking the cowman was still unconscious because his eyes were closed and his breathing was ragged and shallow. Then the old man spoke, startling them both.

"Holmes? . . . You hear me, Holmes?"

Russ dropped down. "I hear you, Mister Campbell."

"Holmes, I've done some terrible things."

"Forget them for now. We can talk later."

"No . . . I got to talk now before my girl gets back. I been listenin' to the lot of you over there by your fire. Holmes; I didn't believe you were square about helpin'. God forgive me for doubtin' so strong and tryin' to kill you so hard."

"He will," said Russ. "So will I. You want some

147

black coffee or a belt of rye-whisky?"

"No. Listen, Holmes; my girl an' my boy'll listen to you. Make my peace for me with 'em an' you can name whatever I got that you want."

Russ looked up at Lefton. Cliff was holding forth his tobacco sack by its little yellow strings. Russ took it, worked up a smoke, lit it and stuck it between old Stuart's grey lips. He then gestured for Cliff to drag up one of the nearby saddles and he propped old Stuart up with this. When those two could look straight into each other's eyes Russ said, "You keep what you've got, Stuart. You've spent a lifetime winning it and keeping it. I'll ride on maybe this afternoon when I've seen you safely home."

Stuart lifted a heavy hand, removed his cigarette and feebly wagged his head. "Don't ride on, boy," he said huskily. "Listen to me a minute. You want that section of south range—I'll give it to you. I'll have your log-house rebuilt. Listen, Holmes; you've got to stay."

Moses Andrews ambled up. He was the only settler still moving around, the others were dead to the world in their blankets. Bearded big Moses exchanged a long, tough stare with old Stuart Campbell and said gruffly, "I just heard what you said, old-timer, and I'm wonderin' if you know just *how* much you owe this feller. He refused to kill you when he could've. He refused to let us kill you too. He even made it possible for you to keep your lousy Tocannon range." Moses shook his head grimly. "In my book, Campbell, you wouldn't be much of a man if you let him ride on."

Old Stuart licked his lips and kept gazing up at Moses Andrews. Ultimately he said, "Help me keep him here, stranger. I aim to make things right again."

But Moses Andrews shook his head and half-turned

148

away. "I wouldn't help you saddle your damned horse," he growled, and went shambling back over where dawn was making the little fire look weak and inadequate as daylight crept softly down the roundabout mountainsides. There, big Moses sat down with his broad back to Stuart and completely ignored him.

Cliff laced a cup of coffee with whisky and brought it to Stuart. The older man sipped it, color came back into his cheeks and he turned drowsy. Cliff and Russ left him propped up quietly resting, went over by the fire and sank wearily down over there.

Petl returned at ten o'clock when the settlers were rousing up and they helped her load old Stuart into the wagon. She waited for Russ and Cliff to then assist the settlers in rounding up their stock, rigging out and afterwards the entire band of them started along towards Tocannon Ranch. They were west of the road near high noon when Cliff sang out, pointing up where Winchester Pass broke out of the hills and struck level valley land. A rider was coming swiftly towards them leading a saddled but riderless horse. They all halted and Russ, studying that horseman, said quietly to Moses Andrews besides him, "Here comes your proof Tocannon Ranch is all deeded property. That's the old man's son, Brigham."

They waited, saying nothing, until Brigham had seen his injured father, had spoken quietly with old Stuart and had afterwards spoken also to his sister. Then he rode on over to Russ, nodded, brought forth a paper from an inside pocket and passed it over.

Russ didn't even open the paper. He handed it to Moses Andrews to read, and it was laboriously deciphered by the burly, bearded settler then gravely and wordlessly returned to Brigham.

"Well?" asked Carl Wendt of Moses. Andrews lifted his mighty shoulders and let them fall. "It's the old devil's land all right. That there is a receipt for a recorded deed. Boys, I reckon we all owe Mister Holmes an apology."

Andrews looked straight over where old Stuart was sitting up in the wagon-bed, his gaze sulphurous. He shook his head bitterly at the older man but he didn't say what he was thinking, which wasn't necessary because they could all read his flinty expression. Then he pushed out a big paw towards Russ.

"Shake," he commanded, and gripped Russ's hand in a bruising grip. "Why don't you do like you said last night—throw in with us? Mister Holmes, ain't a man here as wouldn't be almighty proud to have a feller like you for a neighbor. Which is more'n I could say for that old he-wolf in the wagon."

Russ colored, caught Petl and Brigham closely watching, and dropped Andrews' hand. "If I decide to," he said, "I'll catch up with you boys before you're out of the valley southward."

Andrews touched his hat to Petl, nodded to Brigham and Cliff, threw old Stuart another sulphurous glare, turned his horse and beckoned to his companions. "Let's head on south," he said. "What's another forty, fifty miles when we've already come a thousand?"

Russ sat a moment watching Andrews ride away. There was a warm feeling in him for that rough-tough old campaigner. Brigham spoke up, bringing Russ's attention back around.

"I found this saddled horse wandering around up in the Pass. There wasn't anyone around so I brought him along."

Russ gazed at the animal and shrugged. "His owner's

locked in your smoke-house at the ranch," he said. "Fetch him along; that gunfighter'll need him to leave the country on."

They resumed their way. Russ rode up beside Petl, Brigham and Cliff Lefton rode further back earnestly speaking, and old Stuart bounced along in the wagon-bed ignored by them all, his expression showing deep-down pain which didn't altogether come from his wounded legs.

Petl said, "Russ; don't go. We'll help you rebuild. Paw's learned his lesson. Please don't go."

He looked down at her from the height of his saddle. "I don't want to," he replied. "I never wanted to stay any one place as badly as I want to stay here, Petl. But it's not for the homestead."

She understood that and where another woman might have blushed or dropped her eyes or changed the subject, Petl Campbell didn't; she held his gaze with her dark-liquid eyes and smiled softly with her lips.

"It's springtime. I can show you all the beautiful meadows and trout streams back in the mountains. I can take you where there's a waterfall."

He said soberly, "I'd like that, Petl."

"If you have to ride on, Russ, wait until the end of summer to do it. Promise me you'll wait until then."

His eyes twinkled down at her. "If I stay that long I'll stay forever."

"Promise me?"

He inclined his head, then he grinned down at her. "I didn't really plan to ride on, Petl. Not unless I could talk you into going with me."

"I'd go," she whispered. "I'd leave tomorrow—only I know you'll love this valley if you'll give it a chance."

"It's not exactly the valley I was thinkin' of loving,"

151

he said.

She smiled. "Springtime is a good time," she said, and held out her hand to him. He took it, squeezed it, then let it go. They were by then within sight of Tocannon Ranch again with a good, golden sunlight around them.

We hope that you enjoyed reading this
Sagebrush Large Print Western.
If you would like to read more Sagebrush titles,
ask your librarian or contact the Publishers:

## United States and Canada

Thomas T. Beeler, *Publisher*
Post Office Box 659
Hampton Falls, New Hampshire 03844-0659
(800) 818-7574

## United Kingdom, Eire, and
## the Republic of South Africa

Isis Publishing Ltd
7 Centremead
Osney Mead
Oxford OX2 0ES England
(01865) 250333

## Australia and New Zealand

Bolinda Publishing Pty. Ltd.
17 Mohr Street
Tullamarine, 3043, Victoria, Australia
(016103) 9338 0666